MISTAKEN IDENTITY

When Emma Meadows met two unknown gentlemen in the plum orchard she guessed one of them was Lord Denver. She disliked his companion on sight. But Lord Denver improved on acquaintance and Emma believed that he returned her affections — until he treated her cruelly. She left the vicarage broken-hearted. Would Richard find a way to change her mind?

FENELLA MILLER

MISTAKEN IDENTITY

Complete and Unabridged

LINFORD
Leicester

First published in Great Britain in 2010

First Linford Edition
published 2010

British Library CIP Data

Miller, Fenella-Jane.
  Mistaken identity. - -
  (Linford romance library)
  1. Aristocracy (Social class)- -Fiction.
  2. Love stories. 3. Large type books.
  I. Title II. Series
  823.9'2–dc22

ISBN 978–1–44480–379–2

Published by
F. A. Thorpe (Publishing)
Anstey, Leicestershire

Set by Words & Graphics Ltd.
Anstey, Leicestershire
Printed and bound in Great Britain by
T. J. International Ltd., Padstow, Cornwall

This book is printed on acid-free paper

1

1814

'Someone's coming. Em, what shall we do? Will we be transported if we're caught here?'

Emma Meadows smiled reassuringly at her younger sister knowing that if *she* reacted as dramatically as Eugenie, what would have been merely an embarrassing encounter might well turn into an unmitigated disaster. She felt her sister pressing close behind and she straightened her spine. Whoever it was, they had no more right to be in Lord Denver's orchards than they.

The sound of male voices approaching through the overgrown and neglected trees meant there was no time for them to hide; they would have to brazen it out. She shoved her hair more firmly under her dilapidated straw bonnet and whispered to her sister, 'Keep your head down, pretend we're village girls; with any luck they will ignore us.'

The branches parted and she was face to face with a smiling blond Adonis who stood six feet at least, and was obviously a gentleman of some wealth, judging by his fine apparel. She couldn't see his companion clearly, only that he was somewhat shorter and dressed in more somber garb.

The blond man spoke, his voice light and teasing. 'Look, Dolly, what do we have here? Two fair maidens up to their knees in stolen bounty.'

Emma felt her cheeks flush. She already had an inkling that this could be none other than the errant Lord Denver himself. Since he had inherited the property and the title from his uncle two years ago, he had been conspicuous by his absence. The grounds had become neglected and the once grand abbey, sadly dilapidated.

Remembering her decision to play the part of a simple country wench she kept her head down and dipped in a curtsy, the shallow basket she had hooked over her arm almost spilling its contents. She glanced from below her lowered lashes hoping to see more of the oddly named gentleman who accompanied Denver.

The man who stepped out from behind his companion was dark in every aspect — his clothes, his countenance, his hair and especially his expression. She had never seen a man so inappropriately named. Looking down his aristocratic nose the man spoke, his voice a patronising drawl that sent a surge of anger around her and she was forced to bite her lips to prevent herself answering inappropriately.

'My dear Percy, these are not poachers as we thought, but thieves nonetheless.' She braced herself, almost expecting him to raise a foppish eyeglass and peer at her disdainfully. 'You have no right to be here, you are trespassers.'

Of course they were trespassing, and had been doing so with equanimity these past few years. The previous Lord Denver had had no objection to anyone helping themselves to his fruit. He had no wish to use it himself as he lived the life of a recluse. As long as no one disturbed him he was happy to ignore the intrusions on to his property and even turned a blind eye to the taking of game.

'Come now, Dolly, let's not be harsh. The fruit is going to waste, we have no wish for the plums, so why not let the matter go?'

The supercilious gentleman shrugged as if bored with the whole scenario. 'On this occasion I am happy to be guided by you, Percy.' He stared hard and Emma was made to feel like a child standing in front of an irate parent. 'You may keep the fruit you have, but do not trespass here again, is that clear?'

The man turned his back, not bothering to wait for an answer and strolled off the way he had come, leaving only the far more pleasant Lord Denver to face them. Emma was at a loss to know why his sour companion could feel it behoved *him* to offer his advice on the matter, but the ways of the aristocracy were unfathomable to her.

'Ignore him. I give you my blessing to help yourself to whatever is here. There will be no workmen employed in this part of the grounds for a while.'

Emma curtsied again. 'Thank you kindly, my lord.' She decided it would be safer not to say any more, it would be hard to disguise the fact that she was gently born if she spoke more than a few words. He nodded and smiled, his face open and friendly, quite unlike his taciturn companion, then he too, vanished through the overhanging branches.

'Well, imagine that? We're the first to meet the new Lord Denver. Papa will be glad he's finally come to take up the reins of the estate. Not before time, mind you, his tenants are in sore need of new roofs and the . . . '

'I beg you, Em, please don't start one of your political rants just now, I couldn't bear it. Quickly, as we've finished what we came to do, let's get home before the horrible one comes back and sneers at us again.'

★　★　★

'Aggie, look what we've got, we have four baskets of plums for you.' Eugenie burst into the large kitchen of the vicarage and dropped her baskets on the table in front of their cook-housekeeper, and dearest friend, Agatha Smith.

'Well, my love, you've both been very busy. I reckon there's enough here to make preserves and some wine for the master.' The elderly lady beamed at the younger daughter of Mr Meadows, the vicar at St Margaret's.

'Now, Miss Emma, what ails you? You look as if you've swallowed a stone.' Emma released the vice-like grip she had on her baskets and forced her mouth to curve.

'Nothing is the matter Aggie, those baskets were heavy, that's all.' She stepped back, rubbing her forearms where the handles had dug in so painfully. 'We met the new Lord Denver. Papa will be pleased to know he's finally here.'

She hurried out of the room, unwilling to discuss the unsettling encounter even with Aggie, who was more like a mother to them than a servant. As she hurried from the back of the house, along uncarpeted passage-ways, she met the only other indoor servant they employed, Jane, who acted as both lady's maid and maid of all work. At the vicarage they all helped with the domestic duties; even her father did his turn by fetching in the coal and logs for the fires.

'Oh, miss, the master has just returned and he's in a right old fluster; he says as you should go and see him right away.'

'Thank you, Jane, I'll go immediately.'

Emma had a shrewd idea what had disturbed her father. He must have heard about the arrival of Lord Denver. He had, like the tenants, been living in suspense for the past two years, waiting to know if his position as the vicar would be confirmed, or if the new Lord Denver would wish to replace him with his own incumbent.

It had been difficult for all three of them since Mama had died five years ago. The annuity she had received from her grandparents had ceased and the meagre amount they were obliged to live on made the fruit from Lord Denver's estate an essential part of their livelihood. They grew all their own vegetables, and had a house cow and fowl, but it was still hard sometimes to feed them all.

She paused outside the study, a large room to the left of the front door which made it convenient for parishioners who wished to visit. She remembered at the last moment that she still wore the apron and bonnet she had donned before her excursion in order to protect her clothes, and she glanced into the one mirror they possessed, which hung beside the front door in the draughty entrance hall, so that anyone entering or leaving the premises could check their appearance was satisfactory. Her hair, after being so rudely crushed under her hat was in total disarray. She quickly smoothed it down, tucking in the errant curls and refastening the pins in the coil out at the back of her head. Papa had told her she was the image of her paternal grandmother, who also had sparkling green eyes and flaming red hair. It was most unfortunate, she had been told many times, that she had also inherited a temper to match her fiery locks.

She tapped on the door and went in without waiting for an answer. 'Here I am, Papa, and I can guess your news. Denver is finally in residence at the abbey.'

The man who turned to face her smiled, making him look younger than his three score years. 'So, my dear girl, you've heard as well; the whole village is atwitter. It seems an army of workmen is to be employed to repair and renovate the building and then a full staff is to be found for the house and grounds.'

'That's good news indeed, Papa. It will give welcome employment in the vicinity. Times are hard for all those working on the fields nowadays.'

'I shall not trouble him with a visit until after the weekend. I am hoping he will attend the service on Sunday and I can introduce myself.' He smiled fondly at his eldest daughter. 'I hope you and Eugenie have something a little more . . . well, a little tidier to wear at church.'

Emma laughed. 'You know we have. This gown is a disgrace, but remember we only have a few decent dresses so when we're working we must wear our oldest clothes.'

She prayed her father would not think to enquire how she had heard the news that the abbey was now occupied again; luckily he must have assumed Aggie had informed her and asked no further questions.

'It will be a relief to have the matter of my position settled, my dear. As you know I have already written to your grandparents, Sir James and Lady Masterson, and they have expressed themselves willing to take you and Eugenie under their wing, if that should become necessary.'

'I've already told you, Papa, whatever happens we must try and stay together as a family. If Mama's parents had wished to be involved in our lives they should have taken an interest from the outset. I have no wish to be taken in as a charity case. Perhaps Eugenie and I could find employment somewhere, we are both well educated, you have seen to that. We could become schoolteachers or take up a position as a governess.

Then you could go and live with Aunt May.'

Her father looked at her, his expression tender. 'If I am living with my sister and you two are working in separate establishments it would not be keeping the family together. My dear, surely it would be better for you and Eugenie to be together, and staying with blood relatives, rather than working with strangers?'

Emma sighed. 'You're right, I'm talking fustian. If we cannot be here together then I must do my best to take care of Eugenie, even if it means going to live with our grandparents who have, as far as we are aware, no wish to accommodate us.'

'Please do not scowl, my love. It might not come to pass. Lord Denver might well allow me to continue here and then no-one will have to move.' He paused, waving to her to be seated and stop prowling around the room. 'However, I think whatever happens, you and your sister must take up their kind offer

12

to introduce you in society. You have little fortune to entice a suitor, but you are both so lovely I'm sure you will receive a suitable offer.'

This was another bone of contention between them. Emma had no desire to be auctioned off to the highest bidder. She wanted to choose her own husband, as had her mother, and marry for love, not profit.

2

Lord Denver was smiling as he emerged from the orchard. If those were village girls, he was the Queen of Sheba. Neither poor clothes nor battered bonnets could disguise the fact that both young ladies were gently born. He was looking forward to seeing them as they really were and dropping them the hint that he recognized them as the village maidens caught stealing his plums. He could hear his companion crashing along behind him, but didn't wait for him to catch up. Much as he loved his younger brother, he found his enthusiasm a sore trial at times and relished his moments of solitude.

He stopped to open the rickety wooden gate that led through a brick archway into the kitchen garden. You could barely see this had once been a place where vegetables had been grown to feed everyone here. It was, like the rest of the grounds, full of weeds and in desperate need of attention. He could not understand why his late uncle, from whom he had inherited both the title and a massive fortune, had been so miserly as to leave his estates in such a poor way.

There was no land agent, had not been for several years, and as he had ridden through the surrounding villages he had noticed the sagging roofs and the lack of whitewash on the walls. The few children he had seen playing were thin and raggedy, no smiles of welcome on their faces. The only place where everyone appeared well fed was in the immediate vicinity of Kesgrave Abbey.

His face was grim as he marched through the ruined vegetable plot and back, past the stables, to the rear of the house. If the grounds and cottages were in poor repair his abode was even worse. There were gaping holes in the roof, dozens of broken panes of glass in the windows, and the old part, the original abbey, was uninhabitable. The floorboards here were rotten, the mullions crumbling and it would take more money than he was prepared to spend to bring it back.

He sighed. He had harboured no wish to be a grand landowner, was quite content with the modest estate he had inherited from his own father ten years ago. He had not expected to inherit the title; as far as he had known there were three healthy cousins, all married, in line before him. However, one by one they had succumbed to various accidents and ailments over the years, without his knowledge, and their progeny had been female.

Now *he* was master of all he surveyed. His days as a major in Wellington's army had been brought abruptly to a halt when the letter informing him of his inheritance had finally caught up with him. It had taken over two years to reach him and he had felt he had no option but to resign his commission immediately and return to England.

After collecting his brother from Oxford he had ridden posthaste to view his new inheritance. He wished he had been aware years ago that he was next in line, for he would have made sure Kesgrave Abbey was kept in better repair and all its tenants taken care of. Obviously his uncle had been too wrapped up in his own misery to send him word.

'Hey, Dolly, wait for me. I hope the rest of the female population in these parts are as pretty as those two. As your heir, I feel I have gained enormously in prestige and importance and intend to make the most of it. You have yet to tell me how much my allowance is going to be. My pockets are to let at the moment, it will be a rare treat to have flimsies to spare.'

'Percy, if you persist in calling me by that ridiculous name I shall be forced to draw your cork. It is all very well for a child in leading strings to use such a diminutive for Adolphus, but we're both full-grown and it is time you used my proper name, or call me Richard if you prefer, it is my middle name after all, and the one I used in the regiment.'

His brother laughed and slapped him on the back, the force of the blow making him stumble forwards. 'You punch me on the nose? I should like to see you try. I am taller than you and half a stone heavier.' The young man had scarcely finished speaking when he found himself flat on his back gasping for breath. 'I say, that was unfair! Using your battleground methods on your only sibling is the outside of enough.'

Richard reached down and, grabbing his brother's outstretched hand, pulled him easily to his feet. He might be lighter and shorter than Percy, but he was battle-hardened, not an ounce of spare flesh on his frame, and he moved with the speed and agility of a man well used to dodging bayonets and sabres.

'Enough tomfoolery, brother. We have work to do. You have a good head on your shoulders when you care to use it, which is why I removed you from university. I have need of your mathematical skills and drawing ability in order to start making sense of this chaos here.'

'It's a good thing you've been left a pot of money, because I think it's going to take every coin you've got to restore this place.'

They walked in through the back door; they hadn't quite got used to the fact that they were lords of the manor now and should not be using servants' entrances. It did not befit their elevated station.

There were two men in the kitchen, both with sleeves rolled up and aprons tied around their sturdy frames. Richard greeted his manservant, Enderby, who had served beside him for the past five years he'd spent fighting against the upstart Napoleon Bonaparte.

'Enderby, have you mastered the infernal contraption that masquerades as a cooking range here?'

The older man grinned, his remaining teeth flashing white in his tanned face. 'I have, my lord, and it's burning up a treat. You'll have hot water and a cooked meal tonight, that I can promise you.'

'Good man. What about you, Mitchell? Have you taken to your duties as a kitchen maid?'

The younger man laughed. 'It makes a change from shoveling sh . . . , begging your pardon, sir . . . from working outside.'

Chuckling, Richard left the two busy at their unaccustomed tasks and headed into the house. The only rooms that were usable, even in summer, were the library and study. The old man had used these two rooms himself, sleeping on the day bed in the library. It had taken no more than a couple of hours to scrub the rooms clean, now all they had to do was locate bed linen from somewhere for them both.

'Come along, Percy, we have to find the things we shall need tonight. You, of course, are young enough to sleep on the floor if necessary but I, in my elevated position as a peer of the realm, insist that I have both bed linen and blankets to cover me.'

He dodged his brother's buffet easily and together they ran up the stairs to begin delving into bedrooms hoping to come across useable bed coverings and pillows.

* * *

The Sabbath dawned bright and clear and Emma took particular care over her appearance that morning.

'I think this gown of sprig muslin looks as fresh and dainty as the day I made it,' Eugenie said as she twirled in front of her sister. 'The lemon wrap of Indian silk is a perfect complement to my outfit and the new ribbons on my best bonnet will complete the ensemble. What do you think, Emma?'

Emma pushed the last pin into her fiery coronet before answering. 'I think you look delightful, my love, as always. I envy you your corn-coloured curls, so much more acceptable in Society than mine.'

'But we would still be known as sisters, Emma. We have the same build, we are both of medium height and slender and our eyes are a perfect match. The squire's son, David Culley, told me that mine sparkled like the most precious emeralds.'

'Well! He had absolutely no right to do so, my dear. Whatever were you thinking, to encourage him to make such familiar remarks?' She was smiling as she spoke and knew her sister would take no offence at her reprimand. 'There, I can do no more. I thank God for the box of Indian silks and muslins that we discovered in the attic. Without them we should be poorly dressed indeed.'

She stood up, shaking out the folds in her high-waisted, pale green muslin gown. She ran the filmy material through her fingers, loving the feel of it;

it was an absolute favourite. She reached over and picked up her Sunday bonnet, a shallow brimmed confection with dark green ribbons and a fetching bunch of cherries attached to one side. She placed it on her head and tied the bow.

'Will I do, Eugenie? Do you think Lord Denver will recognize us as the village girls he caught stealing his plums the other day?'

Her sister giggled. 'I doubt it. Dressed as we are, we look as fine as anyone in the neighbourhood.' She raised the hem of her gown and stared gloomily at her sensible brown walking boots. 'I do wish we had sufficient funds to buy pretty footwear too. These boots are hardly attractive, are they?'

'No, but they're practical. We have half a mile to walk to church and fancy slippers would be ruined in no time. Of course, if we could afford a carriage, then we could have dozens of pairs of slippers to go with it.'

Laughing they ran down stairs

together to be met by Aggie and Jane, also in their best, who were going to accompany them. Word had spread throughout the village that the new occupants of the abbey were finally in residence and everyone, even the reluctant attendees, were going to put in an appearance at matins that morning.

'Come, the bells have just started ringing. We don't want to be late, not today.' Emma pulled on her gloves and slipped her reticule strap over her wrist, adjusted her shawl, checked her appearance in the mirror by the door and, with her sister at her side and their two servants behind them, left the vicarage.

* * *

Lord Denver was in his shirt sleeves and stockings, perched on the roof of the abbey. He heard the church bells and swore loudly. He realised at once he had committed a near fatal *faux pas* by failing to attend church on his first morning as lord of the manor. He knew with absolute certainty that the congregation would be expecting him to appear, that they would have turned out in their finery especially for him. They had been without an overlord for far too long and at this, his first obligation, he had failed miserably.

It was too late to scramble down through the attic, change and ride to church. It was better not to go at all than arrive late. He would go to Evensong; at least he could meet Mr Meadows, the incumbent. He shrugged and shouted down through the hole in the roof to his brother who was in the attic below.

'I shall need some more timber up here, the battens are rotten and will not hold the tiles when I replace them.'

A few moments later the tousled head of his sibling appeared beside him. 'Here you are. Do you have sufficient nails?'

He did, and for the next hour he continued to repair the largest hole in the roof. This one let water into the main bed chambers which stood below the attics, and it was these rooms he wished to get back into use as soon as possible. He had been perfectly comfortable stretched out on the day bed in the study, but before he could start employing the staff he needed to repair and run his massive house he believed it wise for both of them to have their own bed chambers. Even he knew that etiquette demanded he should not be seen prowling around downstairs in his unmentionables.

* * *

'How rude of them not to put in an appearance this morning, Emma. I had thought his lordship would have known better than to absent himself, today of all days.'

'So you have said several times, my dear, and I have agreed with you on every point. However, we know nothing about Lord Denver; perhaps he is not cognizant of his obligations? As it took over two years for him to arrive here, it's possible he was unaware that he was next in line.' Emma stopped abruptly. 'Yes, I'm sure that is what it is. He must have been a commoner, a distant relative of the late Lord Denver, and had had no expectations of inheriting the title.'

'Also, he's scarcely older than I am. I put him at about three and twenty, what do you think?'

'About that, yes. His companion was considerably older, I would say nearer thirty than twenty. He was a supercilious gentleman, do you think he might have been his tutor? He certainly had an air of authority and Denver did not seem to mind him giving orders in his stead.'

Eugenie had rushed ahead, swinging her bonnet in one hand and obviously hadn't heard her comments. Emma wished her sister was a little less volatile, but she supposed it was part of her charm and, as Eugenie was still three years from her majority, she had no reason to be staid and solemn.

Since Mama had died it had been her role to run the house and take care of her younger sister. Her father was a kind man, and a good pastor to his flock, but he had no head for figures. If things were left to him they would be sadly in debt. She sighed, then laughed at herself. She was doing far too much of this lately; it was time she accepted that at four and twenty she was past her prime and try and devote her remaining years to looking after her father and acting as his chatelaine.

She couldn't understand why an image of the dark-featured friend of Lord Denver kept slipping into her head at the slightest opportunity. She would, in future, remain fully occupied and then she would have no time to dwell on this unpleasant stranger.

3

It was just after seven o'clock when Emma put down her basket of mending. 'I shall go and make the tea, I heard Papa on the path. Are you going to join us tonight, Eugenie?'

Her sister had been gazing across the room lost in thought and didn't respond immediately.

'Eugenie?'

'I beg your pardon, did you say something? Were you asking me about tea?'

'I was, my dear. Papa is home, I heard him coming in a moment ago.'

'It is far too warm tonight for tea, I should like some lemonade, if there is any left, thank you.'

Emma hurried from the room and met her father crossing the flagstone hall looking far more relaxed than he had for months.

'Emma, my dear, Lord Denver came to Evensong. I was disappointed he didn't appear this morning, as were the rest of the congregation, but in fact it was far better for him to come when it was less crowded as we had sufficient time to converse in peace after the service. Lord Denver is quite content for me to continue in this living as long as I should wish to do so. And, believe it or not, he has doubled my stipend!'

Emma was stunned. Such largesse! They would be able to replace their undergarments and there were several household items that she was desperately in need of too. 'That's wonderful, news. I knew he was going to be an asset to the community as soon as I saw him. I am sorry that I wasn't there to hear the good tidings, but no doubt I shall have ample opportunity to meet him at a later date.'

Her father reached out and took her hands, giving them an affectionate squeeze. 'Indeed, my love, I have invited him to dine with us tomorrow so you shall meet him sooner rather than later.'

Talking happily together, they headed for the drawing-room. 'Go in and tell Eugenie, Papa, she will be as delighted as I am. I shall fetch the tea; I think tonight we shall have a slice of Aggie's plum cake to celebrate.'

She could hardly believe that the financial worries of the past few years were at an end. If their income was to double they would have more to spend than ever before. There would be sufficient to take on a maid of all work, a kitchen maid to help Aggie, and Jane could become their abigail; the girl could take over the mending and sewing that occupied most of their spare time. She would also be able to employ an outside man to help old Fred, who struggled to do more than take care of the cow, the hog and the domestic fowl. Good heavens! Maybe now they could even afford to keep a pony and trap.

'Aggie, we should like to have plum

cake with our tea tonight; from now on you shall have a girl to help you . . . '
She stopped, the room was empty, she was talking to herself. The kettle hissed gently on the range and the tea tray was laid out as usual, but there was no sign of Aggie or Jane. It was not like either of them to wander off when they knew their services were required. She went to the back door and on stepping out into the yard could hear the sound of voices coming from the cowshed. Relieved, she realised that Buttercup must have calved and the two women had gone out to admire the new arrival. Well, that was one worry less. It was always an anxious time waiting for a calf, even with such an experienced mother as Buttercup.

She went back to the range and, wrapping the handle of the kettle in a thick cloth, she lifted it carefully and tipped the contents into the teapot. The aromatic steam rose, filling her nostrils and reminding her of her mother, who had loved this particular blend of tea.

That's another thing: from now on we can have as much tea and coffee as we want. She fetched the lemonade from the pantry for Eugenie, added three generous slices of cake, and returned to the drawing-room to plan with the rest of her family how they could best spend the extra funds.

* * *

Lord Denver was strolling back to Kesgrave Abbey with his brother, well satisfied with the evening's excursion. 'Mr Meadows is an intelligent man, I'm lucky to have him as the rector here. I shall be glad to be able to ask his advice on what needs doing most urgently in the parish.'

'That's all very well, Richard, but whatever possessed you to accept his invitation to dinner? Imagine how it will be, him prosing on, indifferent food and not enough wine to wet my whistle.'

'I could hardly refuse, it's my duty to meet his family and I'm sure the meal will be palatable and the company perfectly pleasant. I don't remember if he said how many children he had, or even if he has a wife; did he speak of either?'

'No, I don't think he did. He might have some pretty daughters to flirt with, that would make the evening worthwhile.'

'You're incorrigible. Do you think of nothing else but young ladies and wine?' He sobered, remembering the last time his brother had overstepped the mark. 'I want your word, Percy, that you will behave yourself tomorrow night. Mr Meadow's daughters, if he has any, are to be left alone.'

★   ★   ★

'The table looks lovely, miss, it's so long since we had the damask out, and the candelabra.' Emma smoothed out the cloth. The last time it had been on dining table was at Christmas five years before, the last Christmas her mother had seen. Mama would be glad that they were finally using it again; it was too fine to be folded up in a chest and ignored. 'Now, Jane, do you understand your duties for this evening?'

'Yes, miss. I'm to greet Lord Denver and his friend, take their hats and gloves and place them on the stand, then I shall conduct them to the drawing-room and announce them.' The girl's brow creased. 'But I don't know the name of his friend, so how can I announce them?'

'Oh, I had not thought of that. Well, don't announce. This is only the vicarage, not a grand house, after all. Just open the door and show them in. Mr Meadows shall give them sherry-wine, if they wish it, and twenty minutes later you must declare that dinner is served.'

Jane giggled. 'It seems a lot of trouble to go to, but I expect that's what fine folks are used to. I can't remember seeing so much food in the kitchen, and all for one meal.'

Emma nodded, proud that she had been able to assemble such a delicious array of local produce at such short notice. Fred had killed a chicken and that was to form the centre-piece of the meal, and she had managed to obtain some trout caught fresh that morning. These would be served poached with dill and parsley. 'We have plum pie and fresh cream, and our own cheese to follow. Make sure that the tea tray is ready for later.'

Satisfied she had done enough, and sure that neither Aggie nor Jane would let her down, she went to check the drawing-room was equally pristine and sparkling before running upstairs to join her sister in the luxury of a bath in the tub placed in front of the fire in her bed-chamber.

At five o'clock precisely she was waiting beside her father and her sister in the drawing-room to greet their guests who were expected momentarily. Excitement fizzed around her body. She knew that they all looked as they should; her gown, and that of her sister's, had been copied perfectly from a recent fashion plate and were as close to the original as it was possible to be. Eugenie was a wonderful seamstress and could produce gowns that were the envy of the village. Her own, of pale green sarcenet over a darker green silk underskirt, suited her auburn hair to perfection. Admittedly the décolletage was a trifle daring, but her mother's emeralds filled the gap admirably.

Eugenie's gown was pale gold with an over-dress of gauze, and even given her bias, Emma believed that her sister looked incomparable. This evening Papa had made an effort, his faded black evening coat freshly pressed, his cravat snowy white and his unmentionables neatly buttoned at the knees. For once, his stockings were unwrinkled and his evening pumps unmarked. This was a miracle for him — he normally had some discrepancy in his appearance.

The sound of voices and footsteps

approaching up the gravel path warned her their guests had arrived. It was barely a mile from Kesgrave Abbey to the vicarage and presumably, as it was such a balmy night, Denver and his friend had chosen to walk.

She wondered what the villagers had made of the appearance of the two gentlemen strolling down the lane dressed in full evening dress. She froze as a horrible thought occurred to her. Would they have bothered to wear formal attire? What if they turned up in day clothes? The three of them would be embarrassingly overdressed, and it was too late to do anything about it now. She looked across at her sister and father, then down at herself. Suddenly, she was no longer pleased with their appearance. They were ridiculously rigged out for a simple meal held in a rustic vicarage. This was not London, she was not a society hostess; what could have possessed them to pretend otherwise?

She heard the front door open and

braced herself, feeling her cheeks flush. The problem with having pale skin and red hair was that she blushed far too easily. She had left the door slightly ajar deliberately; sometimes it stuck, and that would never do tonight. The door opened the rest of the way and Jane, in fresh white cap and apron over her best blue dress, curtsied and stood back to let their guests enter. Her father, never one to stand on ceremony, bustled forward hand outstretched in greeting.

'Lord Denver, and Mr Tennent, you are most welcome here. Allow me to introduce you to my daughters.'

Emma was slowly recovering her composure having seen that both men were as overdressed as they, but wearing trousers rather than knee britches and stockings. She smiled at Lord Denver, looking handsome, his golden hair falling across his forehead, his intricate cravat held in place by a single diamond pin. To her astonishment it was the shorter, older gentleman that her father was addressing.

'May I present my eldest daughter, Emma, and this is her younger sister, Eugenie.' Emma's knees almost buckled beneath her. Of course! How could she have been so stupid — the reason the dark man had given the orders was because *he* was Lord Denver and the younger man his brother. She sank into a deep curtsy, glad that her legs did not let her down. Gracefully she rose and raised her head expecting to see the same patronising smile flickering around his mobile mouth. She received her second shock of the evening.

Lord Denver was staring at her a stunned expression on his face; she watched him swallow as if nervous, but surely that could not be? Then he bowed and his mouth curved into a smile of such devastating charm that for the second time in as many minutes her knees threatened to abandon her. How could she have thought this man austere and supercilious?

She was hardly aware of her introduction to Mr Percy Tennent or of her sister's reaction to the younger man's attentions. She was to bitterly regret this lapse.

4

Conversation at the dinner table was lively and Emma became so engrossed in the discussion about the iniquities of the Corn Law and the agricultural unrest that was spreading throughout the country, that she didn't notice that her sister and Lord Denver's brother were conducting their own, far more personal conversation.

The first course was cleared and the second was placed in front of them. She saw Lord Denver exchange a smile with his brother and her cheeks coloured with annoyance. If there was one thing she disliked above all others it was being excluded from a private jest.

He saw her looking at him and grinned apologetically. 'We had not expected such a splendid repast, Miss Meadows. I had no idea that a country parson set such a good table.'

She could see his eyes glinting with amusement, so responded in kind. 'Indeed, my lord, if you had come last night you would have had bread and dripping for your supper. However, I have called in a deal of favours and Mr Meadows sent out to the squire for some claret and there you are. A meal fit for a king.' She smiled at him. 'Well, for a lord and his brother anyway.'

She waited until Jane had set out the freshly baked plum tart and put the jug of thick cream beside it, then next to that a large wedge of their own cheese and a basket of early apples. There was also a blancmange made with raspberries picked yesterday from the garden, and to complete the array a dish of hothouse peaches, also a gift from the squire.

Her father beamed around the table; Emma could see he was happy that his guests and his beloved daughters were in such high spirits. 'My lord, what can I serve you with?'

Lord Denver smiled enigmatically at

Emma and then gestured towards the pie. 'A slice of that, if you please, sir, for plums are my favourite fruit and freshly picked ones especially.'

Emma bristled. He had known all along — had recognized her as soon as he'd come in, indeed had very probably known them not to be as they purported at the time. Well, he was not going to cause her further embarrassment. She would turn the tables neatly on him.

'Yes, my lord, these very plums were picked from your own orchards. My sister and I collected them the other day.' She heard a gasp from Eugenie and her father dropped the silver knife he was wielding. She waited a moment before continuing blithely. 'The previous Lord Denver gave the village permission to help themselves to fruit and vegetables as they wished. He had no desire for it and was not one to see things going to waste.' She raised her head and stared directly at Lord Denver. He was no longer smiling, but looking watchful, waiting for her to finish. 'In fact, my lord, the only way your tenants have managed to survive these past few years is because they could eat freely from the estate, including any rabbits and game they could find.'

His mouth thinned and he sat straighter in his chair. 'I see.' He ignored her and addressed his remarks to the end of the table, to her father. 'Could I ask you, sir, to include in your sermon on Sunday, that the estate is no longer available for poaching and stealing. As I am not only the landowner but also the nearest magistrate, I shall not look kindly on anyone who ignores the law.'

Emma lost her appetite. She dropped her napkin abruptly and stood up. Eugenie had no choice but to follow. 'I shall leave you gentlemen to finish your dessert and take port, if that is what you wish. Eugenie and I shall be on the terrace.'

Without waiting for an answer she

swept from the room, head held high, her lips pressed together to stop herself from further intemperate and disrespectful responses. She stalked down the length of the drawing-room and out of the open doors at the end. She could hear her sister behind, but didn't stop until she was walking briskly towards the rose garden.

'Please wait a minute, Emma. We shall ruin our gowns if we continue in this way. Although the ground is dry, it's dusty underfoot. It would be far better to stay on the terrace and wait for the gentlemen to join us.'

She was going to refuse, to continue her headlong rush to her favourite place on God's earth, constructed in the very centre of the garden, where she could curl up on the wooden seat and be alone with her thoughts. But . . . 'You're right, Eugenie. I beg your pardon for forcing you to leave the table so precipitously. That man is impossible! He has only been here two days and already he is threatening to incarcerate the local population for doing what they've been allowed to do these past ten years.'

'I know, Emma, but flying up in the boughs at him has not helped the matter, has it?'

Emma turned to face her sister, her anger gone as quickly as it came. 'When did you become the peacemaker, my love? It's usually you that needs restraining from impetuous behaviour.'

Eugenie giggled and threaded her arm through hers. 'I was so shocked to discover that Mr Tennent was not Lord Denver, were not you?'

'Of course I was. The wretched man recognized us at the outset.'

'Yes, of course he did, Mr Tennent told me so. He is a charming gentleman, don't you think, Emma? I believe that he was at Oxford finishing his studies in architecture, but Lord Denver fetched him here to draw up the plans for the improvements to the abbey. Mr Tennent intends to be here for the next few months at least.'

'I do not object to Mr Tennent, he's everything he should be. It is his obnoxious brother who ruffles my feathers. In your conversation with Mr Tennent did you discover why his lordship was so tardy in arriving here to take up his duties?'

By this time they had returned to the terrace, the early evening breeze cooling her overheated cheeks. Emma settled on to a cushioned settle, her sister beside her.

'Yes, in fact he did; he said that Lord Denver was a major in some regiment, I forget the name, fighting against Bonaparte. It took all this time for the letter informing him he had inherited Kesgrave Abbey to find him. It seems he had no idea he was next in line as when he had gone abroad he still had cousins aplenty ahead of him.'

'I thought as much, but if he was a commoner, why is he so arrogant?' She frowned and then answered her own question. 'I believe it must be because he's used to commanding men. A soldier is a different kind of creature altogether to a normal person.'

She couldn't help herself recoiling at the thought that the urbane gentleman, at this very moment contentedly munching his way through a slice of plum tart, had blood on his hands; indeed, had wounded and possibly killed dozens of men in his lifetime.

She hated violence of any sort, would stop a pair of urchins squabbling in the street if she passed them. She understood the necessity for stopping the upstart Frenchman but wasn't sure if she would ever feel comfortable with a man who had killed for his living, however noble his motives. The sound of voices coming towards them ended their conversation and she schooled her features into one of welcome and rose to her feet to greet them.

★ ★ ★

The walk home seemed longer, Richard thought morosely. His spirits were low, the evening had not ended well. Why had he let his damnable temper cause friction between Miss Meadows and himself? He felt a tightening in his chest as he pictured her, the epitome of everything that was lovely. From the tip of her delicate toes to the crown of her glorious head, she was the woman he'd spent half his life looking for. Miss Meadows was kind and intelligent, witty and brave, and from what her father had told him, she had held the family together following the death of her mother.

He kicked viciously at the stone in his path and the pain shot through his unprotected toe making him yelp out loud and swear volubly. 'I had forgotten I wasn't wearing boots, serves me right for being such a curmudgeon.' It was only then he noticed his brother was in particularly high spirits; the strained atmosphere of the second part of evening had obviously not affected his enjoyment.

'Miss Eugenie sings like a nightingale, don't you think, Richard? And

Miss Meadows plays beautifully. It was a delightful evening, far better than I could have imagined. Delicious food, adequate wine and the company of two diamonds of the first water. What more could a man ask for?'

Richard was forced to smile — his brother still found enjoyment in simple things. Perhaps he should try to be more like him, less serious, but he feared his years spent observing the true horror of war had hardened him to frivolity.

'I agree, it was a most enjoyable evening. I look forward to inviting them all back here as soon as the place is fit for visitors.'

* * *

So the weeks passed and Kesgrave Abbey was slowly returned to its former glory. The grounds were scythed to within an inch of their lives, the orchards pruned, the fences mended and the villagers firmly excluded. They might have resented being unable to supplement their table from the bounties of the estate had not Lord Denver offered employment to anyone who required it.

Emma saw the changes happening daily. Peg tiles were replaced, dilapidated cottages repaired, the walls lime-washed, the dirt floors replaced with timber. The village shops and tradesmen found their businesses booming. Every able-bodied man was now working, either in the grounds, or as grooms, footmen or gardeners. Their womenfolk sent their daughters to the abbey to become whatever was required.

She was so busy helping her father, accompanying him in the new pony and trap they had been able to purchase, that she had little time to supervise her sister. She often left Eugenie with a list of instructions and the tasks were always completed without complaint by the time she returned. They now employed two more indoor staff, a kitchen maid, and maid of all work; a sturdy lad from the village had joined Fred outside and two equally ancient villagers were now employed on a daily rate to do the gardening.

It was the end of October. The nights were drawing in, the harvest gathered, and thoughts were turning towards the coming winter when she finally had time to take stock of their change in circumstances. The three of them were sitting cosily in the drawing-room, a roaring log fire in the grate, all lost in their own thoughts.

'Papa, are you sure we have not overspent? You have agreed to every suggestion, every expense that I put before you; I have been adding up the accounts and it comes to a frightening amount of money.'

'Don't fret yourself, my love. His lordship has been most generous. I had meant to tell you, but we have both been so busy these past weeks, that I quite forgot you didn't know what he has done for us. He had the increase backdated to the time that he became owner of the estate. Was that not a liberal thing to do?'

Emma was stunned. 'Then, I shall be sanguine and just enjoy the unaccustomed luxury of having funds to spare. Eugenie, we must go into Ipswich before the weather becomes cold and replace the items of clothing we were discussing the other day.'

'Mrs Busby was telling me at church last Sunday that the Emporium has recently had a delivery of material. If we go immediately there might still be some left. Jane and I can start making us new gowns for the festive season.'

'Then we shall do so, Jane must come with us, and Papa, you must make a list of anything you have need of also.'

Her father beamed and patted his pocket. 'I forgot to tell you girls, today I received an invitation from Kesgrave Abbey — we are invited to dine next Friday. There is to be a ball afterwards, and everyone in the neighbourhood of any consequence will be there.'

Her initial reservations about Lord Denver had long since dissipated and Emma couldn't help a thrill of excitement at the prospect of attending an event of such importance, and of being able to appear looking her best for the man she'd come to regard with such warm affection. She and Eugenie had attended several subscription balls over the years at the local market town where there was a moderately sized assembly room, but they had never been invited to an event like this.

'In that case, it's imperative that we go to Ipswich tomorrow. Eugenie, do you think that you and Jane can make us suitable gowns before next Friday? We only have the one evening dress each and both Lord Denver and Mr Tennent have already seen those.'

'I'm sure we can. Papa, do you think we could have slippers and matching gloves as well?'

'You shall have whatever you want, my dear. You have both been most uncomplaining during our years of hardship, and I shall not stint you now that we have plenty.'

Friday came around almost too soon — the final stitches in their outfits were only placed that very morning. Emma and Eugenie were ready to leave half an hour before the carriage from the abbey was due to collect them. Mr Tennent had called in the previous day to tell them Lord Denver was arranging for transport, as he did not wish them to walk even such a short distance in the dark.

Over the weeks Mr Tennent had been a regular go-between for his brother and her father, fetching and carrying willingly, bringing questions and queries and returning with their answers. When the young man wasn't busy with his drawings he seemed to be always at the vicarage under one pretext or another. Emma was unsure of her feeling towards him. She tried hard to like him, but thought him a little too easy in his manners and much preferred the formality of his brother. She had not had many opportunities to spend time alone with Lord Denver, but they had conversed after matins each Sunday, and he had called at the house and taken afternoon tea with them several times.

'I feel like a duchess, this is the most beautiful gown in the world.' Eugenie spun round, the gold spangles on her over-dress catching the candlelight and the hem lifting to show dainty gold evening slippers.

'Stand still, Eugenie. If you catch your heel in the hem of your dress you will tear it.' Emma's words were enough to restrain her sister, and the glittering skirts settled in a more decorous fashion about her ankles.

'Are you not excited, Em? Neither of us has seen the abbey since it has been restored. I can't wait to see what they have done.'

Emma refrained from pointing out that they'd never seen the inside of the abbey, restored or otherwise. 'As you see, I am beside myself with anticipation,' she said dryly. 'The carriage will be here shortly, do you have spare pins and a handkerchief in your reticule? You have forgotten nothing?'

Her sister tapped her fan on the end of her nose. 'I think I am absolutely ready. Emily told me last week, when she visited with the squire, that I should be wearing pastel colours. It seems that unmarried girls are not supposed to wear either gold or emerald green.'

'I am at an age, Eugenie, when I can wear what I please. And when I saw this silk, the exact shade of my eyes, I could not resist. You have made our gowns so beautifully, no one could possibly know they haven't come from a top modiste in Town.'

She arranged the matching wrap around her shoulders, confident she looked her best. What was keeping Papa? She could hear the crunch of wheels outside. She turned to call her father. 'The carriage is here, are you ready to leave, Papa?'

To her consternation her father appeared still dressed in navy blue topcoat, sadly creased britches and dusty boots. He wasn't ready.

'I'm sorry my dears, but I have been feeling unwell this afternoon. Nothing to worry about, a touch of fever, but I do not feel I can accompany you this evening.'

Emma immediately began to remove her gloves. 'In that case, Papa, we shall not go either. We shall stay here and take care of you.' She saw Eugenie's mouth turn down and knew her sister was going to refuse.

'My dear, I have Aggie here to take care of me. I should have told you earlier, but I was waiting to see how I did. Now, I shall away to my bed, and you go and enjoy yourselves; you have Jane to accompany you, and you shall be among friends. I'm sure there will be no need to have a chaperone.'

Emma was certain that going unaccompanied to such an event was a recipe for disaster. A young lady's reputation was the most precious thing she had and she feared that such forward behaviour would tarnish them in the eyes of the neighbourhood. Eugenie, however, was already on her way down the path, apparently determined to go on her own if necessary. The feeling of eager anticipation Emma had been experiencing over the past few days at the thought of attending this prestigious occasion had vanished like morning dew at sunrise, but she had no option. Hurriedly, she embraced her father and followed her sister from the vicarage. Both Jane and Eugenie were already settled in the carriage, and the liveried footman bowed and offered his arm. The young man spoilt the moment by grinning.

'You look a treat, Miss Meadows.'

It was Jack, the blacksmith's son, almost unrecognizable in his finery. They had known each other from the cradle and his friendly comment helped to stem her growing anxiety. Should she tell her sister that what they were doing was outrageous? That she believed everyone would think they were unfeeling, undutiful daughters and would have done better to stay at home and care for their ailing parent and not parade around in their finery, unaccompanied by a suitable chaperone.

As if reading her mind, Eugenie said plaintively, 'I know we should have stayed, Emma, but we might never have this opportunity again. These gowns have been made specially for tonight, and I could not bear it if no one saw us wear them.'

Emma forced herself to relax. 'I fear this is a mistake, my dear, but it is too late to repine so I shall try and be like you and enjoy the moment, whatever the consequences.'

5

The abbey was flanked by flaming torches, making the whole scene like something from a fairytale. In spite of her misgivings Emma began to feel some of her initial excitement returning. Maybe tonight would not be such a disaster after all. The carriage pulled up in front of the imposing marble steps that led to the entrance of the modern wing.

'Emma, I'm so happy to be here, I can hardly believe so much has happened since we met Lord Denver and Mr Tennent in the plum orchard all those weeks ago.'

'Well, we appear to be the first to arrive, which is fortuitous as now there shall not be a crowd of people observing the fact that we are alone.'

'Fiddlesticks to that! Papa would never have allowed us to attend tonight if there had been anything improper about our doing so. After all he *is* the vicar.'

Emma was forced to smile. Her sister was probably right, if her father was sanguine, then so must she be. 'Remember, Eugenie, we must stay together unless one of us is dancing and then the other must remain with Jane.'

'Emma, I'm not a child. I have been out these past two years and know how to go on at functions such as this.'

Emma doubted the veracity of that statement, but there was no time for further conversation as the carriage door was opened with a flourish and a liveried footman flicked down the steps. He stood with his arm raised to assist them to alight.

Emma walked together with her sister, holding up the hem of her evening gown to avoid both tripping, or miring the material. As she entered the hall she halted in amazement. The hexagonal space, with its black and white chequered floor, was ablaze with what seemed like ten thousand candles. Several massive chandeliers hung from the ceiling, their crystal drops sparkling like gemstones in the light. She gazed round in delight. Her attention was drawn towards the two men watching closely to see their reaction.

'Good evening, Lord Denver, Mr Tennent.'

She sank in a deep curtsy, hearing the rustle of silk as her sister did the same behind her. Before she could straighten an ungloved hand appeared, pulling her gently upright; she felt the heat, the hardness of his fingers as they enfolded hers through her silk gloves and she shivered. He raised her hand to his mouth, his blue eyes blazing into hers, then pressed a gentle kiss across her knuckles sending a second frisson of excitement rushing up her arm.

She was transfixed. She knew she should say something, but couldn't break the spell he was casting over her. She forgot about Eugenie, about behaving with propriety, all she could think about was the man standing, magnificent in black evening dress, in front of her.

'You are most welcome, my dear Miss Meadows. I ensured that you arrived before the others, as I wish to give you a conducted tour of my home; you have been so closely involved with the renovations I feel it only right you should be the first to see the result.' It was only then he noticed they were unaccompanied. 'Mr Meadows is not with you?'

Emma laughed out loud. 'Obviously not, my lord. He has a touch of fever and was unable to be with us this evening. He sends his apologies.'

'I'm relieved to hear that he is not seriously ill. I shall call in to see how he does tomorrow morning. Now, my dear, are you ready for your tour?'

'That would be most acceptable, thank you. I have to own that this is my first visit inside Kesgrave Abbey so I fear it might be difficult for me to judge if the place has actually been improved by the work.'

Lord Denver chuckled at her sally and threaded her hand into the crook of his arm. 'In that case, Miss Meadows, you must endeavour to be massively impressed by whatever you might see.'

Emma belatedly remembered her sister and glanced quickly over her shoulder; she saw to her consternation that Mr Tennent, Eugenie on his arm, was disappearing in the opposite direction to themselves. She gestured to Jane to follow; she didn't trust that young man to be alone with Eugenie without taking advantage of her inexperience.

Emma's mouth curved involuntarily — although she might be six years Eugenie's senior, she had as little real knowledge of the world. However, what she lacked in experience she more than made up for in commonsense. She turned back to her escort. 'I apologise for my inattention, sir, I was a trifle anxious to see my sister leaving unattended with Mr Tennent.'

His mouth tightened and his eyes

narrowed at her words. He saw that the young couple were going into the drawing-room together, Jane almost running in order to follow them. He nodded in approval at that.

'She has her abigail with her, Miss Meadows, so all will be well.'

He conducted her from chamber to chamber, indicating points of historical interest — the magnificent mullioned windows, the family portraits — and eventually they returned via a different route to the entrance hall.

'That was most educational, my lord. I had no idea this place had had so many additions over the centuries, though I must admit I much prefer this modern section. The ceilings are so much higher and the windows beautifully proportioned to let in the maximum light.'

Before he could answer she heard the sound of carriage wheels arriving outside the open front door. The two liveried footmen, more young men from the village, jumped to attention and Richard smiled ruefully down at her.

'I fear that duty calls, Miss Meadows. But rest assured I shall be monopolising you for the rest of the evening.' He snapped his finger and a third man-servant appeared from the shadows. 'Take Miss Meadows through to the drawing-room, and find Mr Tennent and ask him to join me here at once.'

The young man bowed and smiled shyly at Emma. 'Would you care to come this way, Miss, there's a grand apple-log fire burning in the drawing-room.' Emma returned his smile. He had yet to learn that servants were not supposed to hold conversations with the guests, but he was another familiar face, so she followed him without comment. She had barely reached the double doors when Eugenie appeared from an adjacent passageway, looking flushed and overexcited — and unaccompanied by either Jane or Mr Tennent.

'Where have you been, Eugenie? You should not be wandering about this place on your own. And why is Jane not with you?'

'Jane is right behind me.' Her sister tossed her head sending the blonde ringlets on either side of her face bouncing. 'I believe that you and Lord Denver have just been doing exactly as we have and you did not have a maid traipsing along behind *you*.'

'You're right, Eugenie, I have absolutely no right to criticise your behaviour. However, I am neither flushed nor over-animated.'

'I promise you Emma, I have done nothing you would disapprove of. I am hot because we were in the billiard room, which is at the far side of the house, when the summons came. I sent Jane to find the whereabouts of the ladies' retiring room. Oh, good, here she is now.'

Their maid appeared looking equally hot and bothered. 'The room we are to use is back the way I've just been. There are two girls to assist in any repairs and everything else you might need has been set out.'

'Thank you, Jane. I should like to

visit now, for it is far too warm to wear this wrap and I need to leave it somewhere safe. Come along, Eugenie, we can rejoin the guests in the drawing-room when we are ready.' Her real reason for escorting her sister quickly into the privacy of the retiring room was that she didn't wish anyone else to see how flushed Eugenie was. 'My dear, do you think you might be going down with the fever like Papa?'

'No, I shall be fine once I have bathed my face.'

Emma turned at the sound of male voices. To her surprise, Lord Denver's brother was standing next to him, about to greet the next arrivals as though he had been there all along. She wondered just how many ways around this enormous house there actually were.

The exalted company gathered in the drawing-room where flunkies waited with crystal glasses balanced on silver trays, some containing champagne, others orgeat. Emma had never tasted the sparkling wine before and found it most enjoyable. When a second glass was offered she gladly accepted it.

She sipped her drink and glanced around the assembled company over the rim. Most were familiar faces, some friends, some merely nodding acquaintances. Emma thought that there must be more than fifty people standing around talking and drinking and still there was space for more. She believed that the drawing-room at the vicarage must fit in this magnificent room many times over.

Eugenie had stayed at her side and they had nodded and curtsied, smiled and chatted for what seemed like an eternity when a formidable gentleman, dressed entirely in black, eventually appeared to announce that dinner was served. A rustle of anticipation ran through the crowd. It was after six o'clock; they were not used to waiting on their meal, everyone kept country hours in Kesgrave.

She turned to Eugenie, not sure exactly where their proper place was in the parade. Towards the tail, she thought, because although they were the grand-daughters of a baronet they were also the daughters of a lowly country parson. She noticed Lord Denver moving easily towards them.

'Miss Meadows, would you do me the honour of accompanying me into dinner?'

She was about to refuse, not wishing to leave her sister alone, when Mr Tennent appeared and made the same request to Eugenie. 'Are you sure there's not someone more important you would rather take?'

'No, my dear Miss Meadows, you are the most important person here this evening.'

Emma's heart skipped a beat at his words and she smiled shyly up at him. 'In that case, my lord, I shall be delighted to be your partner.'

In spite of her happiness she was aware of the narrowed eyes and basilisk stares that greeted her sudden eleva-tion. The village tabbies would make much of this; she and Eugenie had better make sure they behaved with impeccable manners tonight, as the slightest slip would not go unnoticed.

He led her down the length of the drawing-room, through the open doors set half way down, into an equally impressive dining-room. The table was large enough to seat the entire company and still leave ample space for the dozens of footmen waiting to help the diners in to their respective chairs. Emma was aware that no name cards had been placed on each setting which meant guests were seated as they arrived at the table. The meal was served *scène a la russe*, the many servants taking the removes around the table and offering them to each diner in turn. There were several courses, each more delicious than the last, before the meal drew to a close. She could scarcely remember what she'd eaten, her entire evening had been taken up with light-hearted conversation with her host and those seated to either side of them.

The nuts and marzipan fancies were on the table, the port ready on the sideboard, when she whispered to Lord Denver from behind her fan, 'My Lord, is it I that must lead the ladies out?'

He grinned. 'Yes, Miss Meadows, but I warn you, do not become too settled, we shall not linger long over the port.'

Emma folded her napkin neatly and stood, catching Eugenie's eye as she did so. Instantly her sister rose, and the many footmen rushed forward to pull back the ladies' chairs. She noticed, with some amusement, that the livery of several servants did not fit as well as it might. Emma surmised that all suitable young men currently employed at the abbey had been dragooned into service as indoor staff for this grand event. They would have been obliged to wear whichever outfit fitted them the best.

She led the throng of twittering ladies back into the drawing-room where the chairs had been rearranged into conversation groups. The wide doors that led through into the ballroom had been opened so the sound of the musicians tuning up could be clearly heard.

'Emma, has your dance card been filled yet? I have already pencilled in Mr Tennent for two dances, and I have only two spaces still free.'

She had quite forgotten about her dance card, it was still in her reticule and completely empty. She had been so busy enjoying the company of Lord Denver she had quite forgotten there was to be dancing later.

'Mine is embarrassingly empty. I shall no doubt be obliged to sit with the older ladies and watch you young girls dancing.'

Eugenie snorted inelegantly. 'Fustian! You know you shall do no such thing. Lord Denver will claim his dances, and there will be a queue of men, both young and old, waiting to write their names in your card as soon as they join us.'

There was a clear space in front of the window at the far end of the drawing-room and so she glided in that direction, pausing to speak a few words to various ladies as she passed by. She gazed out across the park, the ghostly shapes of trees etched in silvery light, the skies a clear navy blue, the stars sparkling overhead just for her.

'Excuse me, Miss Meadows, Mama and I were so admiring your gown. Such an unusual colour for an unmarried lady. Did you have it made locally?'

Emma forced her lips into a smile as she turned to answer the barbed compliment from the daughter of a wealthy neighbour of Lord Denver's. 'Thank you so much, Miss Carstairs, for your kind enquiry. We were also admiring your gown, were we not, Eugenie? Rose is such a becoming colour for a brunette, and the abundance of flowers sewn so daintily around the hem and neck line are quite charming.'

Emma felt Eugenie quiver and hoped she would be able to maintain a straight face. The young lady in question was dressed in the height of fashion, but like many others present had decided that adding more flowers, ruffles and ruches to the neck and edges of their gowns could only make them better. They were sadly mistaken in her opinion.

The young woman simpered. 'Mama and I went to Town to obtain *my* wardrobe. We shall be going up for the season in February; shall we see you and Miss Eugenie this year?'

'My sister and I do not attend the London season. We are the daughters of a country parson and have more serious duties to attend to than such frivolities as parties and soirées.'

She could hear Eugenie choking quietly behind her, and knew that she had said too much as usual. Miss Carstairs was not sure if she had been insulted or flattered, but curtsied briefly and returned to her mother, watching beadily, resplendent in lilac taffeta and a matching turban liberally decorated with ostrich plumes.

Emma felt a ripple of anticipation run through the room and knew that those nearest to the dining-room doors had heard sounds of movement from within. The gentlemen were about to join them. The small orchestra was already playing a lively jig and she could see Eugenie was not the only one eager to go through and dance. The doors opened and the gentlemen appeared, some, like Lord Denver and his brother, in the modern fashion of trousers and evening slippers, but others still wearing knee britches and stockings. Most were in black-and-white, but a few older gentlemen still favoured the flamboyant colours of an earlier era.

Lord Denver and his brother held her attention and that of every other single lady present. Mr Tennent, tall, fair and handsome, his brother dark and commanding, both with flashing blue eyes — who could possibly resist such an attractive, and wealthy, duo?

Her heart flipped as her host headed directly for her. He clicked his heels, nodded his head and held out his hand.

Emma stared at it foolishly.

'Your dance card, Miss Meadows. I believe I have to write my name upon it.' Obediently she removed it and handed it over, watching him sign his name in a bold, black scrawl in three spaces — opening set, the supper dance and the final waltz. He handed it back with a smile that turned her knees to water. Should she protest that he had claimed one too many?

'I believe this is my dance. Miss Meadows, shall we lead the company out on to the floor?' The rest of the evening rushed by in a carrousel of music and laughter. Both she and Eugenie danced every dance with a motley collection of partners, both young and old. The German waltz had only recently arrived in England and this would be the first time she had danced it in public. It was to be the final dance and she could hardly wait to be held in *his* arms and twirled around the floor in front of the assembled crowd.

She had told Jane to stay close to her sister at all times. She, herself, was sensible enough to avoid being trapped into anything indelicate. Eugenie, however, was headstrong and incautious and could well cause a scandal if not watched carefully. They had agreed to meet immediately after the waltz as their carriage, Lord Denver had informed her, would be the first to arrive.

'This is my dance, Miss Meadows. It's the one I have been eagerly anticipating all evening.' He took her hand and guided her to the very centre of the ballroom. As the orchestra struck up the first bars, he gently placed his arm around her waist whilst she rested hers on his shoulder. She felt uncomfortable so close to him, and could feel the heat of his hand through the thin silk of her dress. For the first few steps she was unsure and almost stumbled.

'Relax, my dear, allow me to guide you; you are an excellent dancer and the waltz is one of the easiest to master.'

She did as he bid and he was right,

within a few moments her feet appeared to find their own way as he guided her expertly around the floor, in and out of the other couples.

'How is it, my lord, that a soldier can dance so well?'

His smile flashed as he answered. 'Wellington demanded that all his officers could dance. We often had to entertain at grand balls and affairs of state.'

'Are you sorry that you missed the final battle of Waterloo? It must be difficult knowing that so many of your regiment were lost there.' She saw his eyes darken and immediately regretted her intemperate words. 'I beg your pardon, my lord, I should not have mentioned such a thing at a time like this.'

For a moment he didn't answer. He gazed over her shoulder, his expression stern.

'No, Miss Meadows you should not. Pray excuse me, I fear I must abandon you. I have to be elsewhere.' His abrupt words fell over her like an icy shower, and her shock was aggravated by humiliation as he unceremoniously abandoned her at the far end of the ballroom and vanished through the open French doors at the rear of the overheated room.

She could feel every eye upon her, many gloating at her downfall, and her burgeoning love turned instantly to loathing. How dare he allow her to be publically disgraced for such a minor infringement of etiquette?

Keeping a false smile on her lips she hurried out of the main doors, which led in to the hall. Where could she go to hid her ignominy? The retiring rooms — in there she could be private and recover her composure before being obliged to face the censorious eyes of the other guests again. When she finally emerged, outwardly calm, she could hear the strains of the waltz continuing in the ballroom. Where should she wait inconspicuously? There were soft footsteps behind her and she turned.

'Excuse me, Miss Meadows, would

you care to follow me to a private withdrawing-room? Your carriage is unavailable at the moment and it would be best if you waited in comfort until it is ready.' The lady, obviously the housekeeper, curtsied politely and waited for her to follow.

Her head was spinning. She feared she had imbibed too much champagne earlier, and having two more glasses of wine with her meal had been a foolish decision. She believed that sitting quietly on her own was exactly what she would like to do. The room was warm, the day bed comfortable and if she closed her eyes, only for a moment, it could do no harm. However the alcohol and her fatigue overcame her and she was soon so deeply asleep she did not even stir when the door opened an hour later.

6

Richard held Miss Meadows as close as he dared. It was for her sake that he had insisted the waltz was included, or how else was he to have a legitimate opportunity to embrace her? She smiled at him; it made him feel like a green boy again, hardly able to form a coherent sentence. In order to compose himself he averted his eyes, staring firmly over her shoulder. What he saw made him forget everything, including his partner.

To his horror he watched Percy dance Miss Eugenie closer and closer to the open French doors and then whisk her through them. If he hadn't been watching at that precise moment he was sure he wouldn't have noticed, and would have thought they were still amidst the many couples whirling around the floor. Emma had said something, but he hadn't heard her. He glanced down, his face still preoccupied, trying to decide how best to handle the situation.

'I beg your pardon, my lord, I should not have mentioned such a thing at a time like this.'

He frowned. He thought they might have been conversing about Waterloo. 'No, Miss Meadows, you should not.' He came to a decision, better to embarrass his partner than have her sister ruined. 'Pray excuse me, I fear I must abandon you. I have to be elsewhere.'

He saw the shock reflected on her face and hated behaving like an ill-mannered brute. He had no choice though. He would explain all to her later, and he was sure she would understand that her sister's safety was paramount. He waltzed her towards the rear exit and stopped. He released her, bowed and turned away, his thoughts on what might be taking place outside the windows, not on what was happening in the ballroom. Where was the wretched maid? He didn't have time to find her, so just hoped she would realise her charge had slipped away without her knowledge and come searching.

The terrace was empty, but the moon was high, filling the grounds with sufficient light for him to see at once that neither of them were anywhere in sight. He heard the sound of female footsteps behind him and prayed it wasn't Miss Meadows following him. What was going to happen would not be pretty and he had no wish for her to see it. He glanced over his shoulder relieved to see it was the girl.

'I'm glad you've come. Have you any idea where they might have gone?'

'No, my lord, I'm that sorry. One minute they were there, the next vanished. It took me a while to realise as there are so many people dancing.'

'Never mind that now. At any time this evening did Miss Eugenie say she had plans to go somewhere with Mr Tennent?'

'No, my lord. She has barely spoken

to me this evening, but I did overhear Mr Tennent saying he had something important to discuss with her and they would need privacy to do it in.'

Richard swore under his breath. 'I knew it. He's up to his old tricks again. This time he shall not succeed. It's time he learnt to take responsibility for his actions.' He was talking to himself, but the young woman muttered a response as she hurried behind him, holding up the skirt of her modest blue evening dress to keep it from the dust.

He ran along the terrace, down the steps towards the back of the building. He had a good idea where Percy was taking his captive. The last time he had seduced a young woman it had taken place in the sweet-smelling hay above the stable block at their old family home in Kent. Fortunately the girl was from the village and had been amenable to a substantial monetary gift and no unfortunate consequences had arisen nine months after the sordid event.

He hurtled round the corner just as

two figures stepped into a pool of moonlight; it was Percy carrying the girl in his arms. He could see at once that she wasn't protesting at this treatment, she was a willing captive. No doubt Percy had suggested that by carrying her he would protect her gown. He didn't dare shout. To do so would alert the many grooms and coach drivers waiting somewhere close by, harnessing their horses and making ready for the end of the evening.

His wretched brother was so engrossed in his seduction that he didn't hear Richard approaching from the rear. With one move, he swung Percy round.

'Put Miss Eugenie down. Do it now.' His voice cut the night like a knife and Percy dropped Eugenie as if she was on fire. He heard Jane arrive behind him and without looking round he issued his orders. 'Take Miss Eugenie in through the side door, and then straight out of the front. The carriage will be waiting. Get her into it and take her home. Quickly, you must go now before anyone else becomes aware of what almost happened.'

Eugenie, unwisely, refused to move. 'How dare you tell me what to do? You are not my guardian. Percy, tell him — we are to be betrothed, isn't that why you asked me to come here with you?'

Richard saw his brother flush painfully, but instead of answering he started to back away. 'Oh no you don't. Stay where you, I haven't finished with you.' The young man froze, not daring to move when he was spoken to in such a fearsome way. 'Have you no more sense than a cabbage, Miss Eugenie? My brother has no intention of marrying you. He had far worse on his mind. This is not the first time he has done this, but believe me, it will be the last. Go with your maid now, there's a good girl, and all might yet be well for you.'

Belatedly he remembered the plight of Miss Meadows. He called out to the maid. 'Jane, make sure that a member of my staff conducts Miss Meadows somewhere quiet to wait for the carriage to return.'

'Yes my lord, I shall do that right away. Come along, Miss Eugenie, we must get you home before everyone comes out of the ballroom.'

He heard the girl gulp, but she didn't break down. She obviously knew that now was not the time for hysterics. If her reputation was to be saved she needed to get herself away before the last waltz finished.

Without another word the two women hurried away. He heard the door open and shut behind them. He swung back to face his terrified brother. He didn't bother to say anything else; he stepped forward and swung his right arm, catching Percy with a massive uppercut. Percy fell, as if pole-axed, without a sound.

Richard blew on his smarting fist and was tempted to follow up his single punch with a few well-aimed kicks. Percy deserved it; he deserved to be thrashed within an inch of his life for what he had been about to do. Eugenie was no village lass, she was gently born and, if Richard had his way, was about to become a member of his family. In the distance he heard the last strains of the music die away. There was the sound of loud applause and shouts for more. The musicians duly obliged and the waltz tune began again. Thank God! This would give him a much needed few minutes more. He had to be in the hall to bid his guests farewell, but he had one more thing to do first.

Racing round to the rear of the abbey he spotted his man, Enderby, sitting at a table reading a newspaper in the servant's hall. He rapped sharply on the window and raised his finger; instantly his man was on his feet, dragging on his top coat as he ran out.

'Good man. Percy's unconscious round the back, near the hay barn. Lock him in somewhere, I'll explain later.'

'There's a store room in the barn,

shall I use that?'

'Yes, he can spend the night in discomfort. He's lucky to be breathing after what he attempted. Being in his cups is no excuse.'

The music was finally drawing to a close — he had a minute to get himself to the hall or all would be lost. Enderby vanished to do his task and he sped back to the side door and went in, pausing to scrub his slippers dry on the end of a convenient curtain then, checking that his cravat was more or less correct and his clothes uncreased, he strolled nonchalantly into the entrance hall just as the first of his guests appeared from the ballroom.

By the time he had bid them all farewell more than an hour had passed and the carriage that had removed Eugenie was back and waiting outside for Miss Meadows. Leaving his minions to douse the candles and remove the worst of the debris, he marched back to the small parlour in which his beloved had been placed.

He tapped on the door quietly, but receiving no answer opened it and stepped in. He stood for a moment staring, his heart full of love. Emma, for that was how he thought of her even though he was not yet in the position to use her given name, had fallen asleep on the *chaise-longue*, her head cradled in her hand, her beautiful emerald green dress spilling out around her.

He shook his head in disbelief. How had it come to this? He was a veteran of the Peninsular Wars, had no time for such flummery, but love did strange things to a fellow and he finally understood what friends had meant when they said they would give their lives for the woman they loved.

It would be best not to wake her if he could avoid it. Explanations would be forthcoming in the morning, better to avoid them now. He spoke quietly to her and shook her shoulder gently, but she didn't stir. He smiled tenderly — he believed her deep slumber more an after effect of too much unaccustomed wine than mere fatigue.

Bending low, he placed her folded arm around his neck, slipped one hand under her knees and the other around her waist. He lifted her easily; she murmured something, he couldn't catch quite what, then settled trustingly against him. He loved the feeling of her face against his shoulder and tightened his hold.

Richard carried his burden swiftly from the house, ignoring the bewildered expression of the remaining footman who was up a ladder dousing the massive chandelier. He scrambled inside the waiting carriage. He should have placed her on the squabs, but chose instead to keep her in his arms. They arrived at the vicarage far too soon.

Jane was waiting anxiously at the door for him to enter. The house was dark, and she held a single candlestick in her hand to light his way up to Emma's bedchamber.

'Place her on the bed, my lord, if you please, then go quickly. It's better that no one knows you've been here.'

'Tell Miss Meadows that I shall call on her in the morning and will explain everything to her then.'

The young woman handed him a candlestick and he crept back down the stairs like a thief. He closed the front door silently, ran down the path and jumped into the carriage, making it rock violently. He had found the woman he wished to marry, but feared that tonight's events might have permanently alienated her and her family. How could she marry him, the brother of a man who had tried to ruin her sister? He collapsed into a corner, glad the darkness allowed him to face his misery unseen.

* * *

Emma awoke disorientated, not sure for a moment where she was. Surely she had closed her eyes stretched out on a daybed at Kesgrave Abbey? How could she now be at home, in her own bedchamber, in her nightgown with her hair loose about her shoulders?

She scrambled out of bed and, pushing arms into her warm bed-robe, decided that she would go and see how Papa fared. What about Eugenie? What had happened to her? She lit a candle from a glowing ember in the fire place and, holding it high, she stole out into the corridor and carefully opened the door of her sister's chamber. She could hear the sound of gentle breathing within and knew that Eugenie was safely in bed; for some reason her sister had decided to leave the party early, taking the carriage, and that was why she had been obliged to wait. No doubt she would hear all about it when her sister appeared to break her fast.

Reassured that the youngest member of her family was safe and well, she walked to the far end of the passage and softly opened door of her father's room. She saw at once he was awake, for a candle burned by the bedside. 'Papa? May I come in?'

'Of course, my dear girl. I was thinking about you both and was about to get out and check that you were home safely.'

'How are you? Has your fever gone?'

'Yes, my love, I am fully recovered. Now, come and sit with me and tell me why you're wandering around in the middle of the night looking so unhappy.'

Emma needed no second urging. She pulled up a small chair to sit on, but before doing so she threw several logs on the fire and gave them a vigorous stir with the poker. Satisfied the room would soon be warm enough, she went to sit by her father and regale him with the events of the previous night. Her father listened patiently until she had finished her sorry tale. 'He's a monster, to treat me so callously. I shall never speak to him again. It's unforgivable; I shall be the talk of the neighbourhood for months to come.'

'I am sure there is an explanation, my dear. Remember we have both come to know Lord Denver well over these past few weeks, he's a good man, his heart is sound. Admittedly, he may be a trifle brusque and overbearing at times, but that is his manner, he means no harm. He was an officer in the army after all.'

Emma rubbed her eyes, staring in disbelief at her parent. How could her father take his side? Didn't he understand the humiliation and embarrassment she had suffered so publicly the night before? 'Lord Denver might be all things you say Papa, but as far as I'm concerned I have no wish to speak to him again, and I believe that his brother has offended Eugenie as well.'

'What do you mean?' Her father's voice was sharp, as if he suspected something untoward might have occurred between Mr Tennent and his younger daughter.

'I mean that Eugenie returned early with Jane, and I was obliged to wait for the carriage to come back for me; that is why I was so much later coming home. She would only have done that if she was distressed by something.'

'I should have nipped it in the bud. I saw the way things were going, but we have both been so engrossed in our own affairs, my dear, that we have let matters come to this sorry state. Your sister imagines herself to be in love with that young man, however, I am uncertain of Mr Tennent's feelings towards her. I cannot believe it credible that he tried to take advantage of her in any way. You know your sister, she takes offence easily. Thank God she had the sense to return home and not make a public scene.'

Emma was not so easily convinced. 'I do not trust him, Papa, he is too glib, too ready to smile at one's witticisms, to flirt outrageously. No, I consider that both Mr Tennent and his brother are both reprehensible. I have no wish to speak to Lord Denver, and I'm sure that Eugenie will not wish to see Mr Tennent either.'

The cockerel in the yard began to crow. The vicarage would soon be bustling with the new maidservants about their duties. 'If you have no objection, Papa, I shall send a letter to our grandparents and finally accept an invitation to visit. We received a letter from them only the other day, and I have not yet replied to it.'

'That's an excellent notion, my dear. If we send the boy to catch the mail coach first thing, your missive should be with them by Monday. I'm sure they will wish to send a carriage directly they hear from you for they have been most pressing in their invitations since your poor mama passed away. This will give you ample time to sort out your wardrobe and pack your trunks.' He reached out and clasped her hands in his own. 'Whatever your feelings, my dear girl, it would never do to run away. Leave with dignity next week and no one shall think you departing for any reason other than an invitation of long standing to spend time with relatives.'

Emma gave her father an affectionate kiss. He was a wise man. 'Thank you, I shall be guided by you. You are the best father alive — we shall both miss you dreadfully. I fully expect to hate it there, but in the circumstances I can think of nothing else. I know what village life is like, some other scandal will occupy the busy tongues before long and then we shall be able to return without being made to feel embarrassed every time we leave home.' She paused at the door. 'I hope we can be excused from service this Sunday, Papa?'

'In the circumstances I can hardly object. We shall have a short service here before I leave for matins.'

She returned to her chamber, pleased that between them they had come up with an acceptable solution, but her head ached and her heart was heavy. How could things have come to this? Yesterday she had been full of hope, believing that her affections were returned, but Lord Denver had made her a figure of fun, rejected her in the cruellest possible way.

Deciding she would get dressed even

though it was scarcely dawn, Emma removed the plainest dress she owned from her closet. Jane appeared when she was halfway through her *toilette*, her face pale and her eyes like dark circles. Emma realised she was not the only one who had suffered a sleepless night.

'Oh, Miss Meadows, what happened last night was all my fault, I should have kept a better eye on Miss Eugenie.'

Emma felt sick; exactly what was Jane talking about? 'What did happen? You had better tell me at once, Jane.'

Too late, her maid knew she had spoken out of turn, but bit by bit she described what had transpired the night before. When she had completed the horrific story, Emma felt such fury she had the urge to hit something, smash something. She wished it was Denver's brother she could strike. She was not a violent person, but she sincerely hoped Lord Denver had thrashed his brother for his perfidy.

'I never trusted him, Jane. But the

blame is not entirely yours, I should have kept a better eye on Miss Eugenie. She thought he was to marry her? How could he have led her along like that? She's an innocent and gently born.'

She closed her eyes, trying to understand the scale of the disaster. She had known Eugenie had returned upset, but in her worst imaginings she could not have come up with the true reason. The stupid girl had been going willingly. If Denver had not stopped them matters would have been so much worse. Eugenie would be a fallen woman, and both their lives totally ruined.

'This debacle was not your fault, Jane, I beg your pardon for inferring that it was. You did everything you could. I understand now why Lord Denver treated me so badly. He was right to do so — to be made a laughing stock is nothing compared to being cruelly seduced.'

She collapsed onto the bed more wretched than before. Being angry, hating a man who had mistreated you, was far easier than feeling as she did now, knowing that her dreams were as ashes. There was no possibility of a match between the man she loved and herself, not now, not after the behaviour of his brother. 'Jane, go and see to Miss Eugenie. If she is feeling up to it, get her dressed and bring her down to the drawing-room.'

The sun was rising, bathing the village in beautiful red light, but she saw none of it. Her heart was broken. She must put her own happiness aside, and think of Eugenie now.

* * *

When Lord Denver came to call later that morning and asked to speak to her, she refused to see him, knowing it was for the best. He spent some while closeted with her father and then left; she heard him striding away, taking her heart with him.

Eugenie was apathetic, too wretched

to have an opinion one way or another about their forthcoming departure. All she said on the matter was that she had been sure Mr Tennent intended to marry her, that he had convinced her it was permissible to be alone together if they were to be betrothed. She berated herself constantly for being so gullible, and swore that she would never fall in love again. Instead, she would become a spinster, a solace to her father in his old age.

'I have no desire to remain here, to be reminded every moment of his betrayal so I suppose we might as well go and visit our grandparents. After all they have invited us often enough these past few years.'

'It will become easier, my love, and because of Lord Denver's quick action no damage has been done to your reputation. We can return in the New Year and carry on as though nothing untoward has happened between the gentlemen at Kesgrave Abbey and ourselves.'

At no time did her father or sister ask how Emma was faring; they must assume that it was only Eugenie who was suffering heartbreak. She had only recently understood herself that she loved Lord Denver and had had no time to share this discovery with her sister before that fateful night. Now it was far too late, and she must bear her grief as best she could in the privacy of her chamber.

7

'I am going to miss you dreadfully, my dears, but it is for the best. It is high time you were introduced to society, you have mouldered away down here quite long enough.'

'Papa, we have no intention of going into society, whatever Sir James and Lady Masterson might think. We intend to pay a family visit, meet our uncle, aunt and cousins and that's all.'

Eugenie had, in the three days since she had learned that Mr Tennent and his brother had left the neighbourhood, become more animated, her broken heart healing far more rapidly than Emma could have hoped.

'Do you think we shall be able to ride? It's so long since we had a horse, here, but I have never forgotten the thrill of being so high or travelling so fast.' She smiled before continuing.

'Mind you, I believe I was only trotting at the time and on no more than a pony.'

The sound of her laughter cheered them all. Emma joined in the merriment. She was glad, of course she was, that her sister's desolation appeared to be a transient thing. Perhaps if she had known this last Saturday she would not have sent Lord Denver away. It was too late now, he had gone, perhaps for ever, leaving a competent estate manager and an army of servants to take care of things in his absence.

The last of their trunks was strapped to the back of the luxurious coach that had been sent for them. She could delay her departure no longer — if they were not to be obliged to stay overnight on the road they would have to leave immediately. Neither of them had ever spent a night away from home before, and she felt like a child must on being sent away to school for the first time. The final embrace from her father was almost too much for her composure and she blinked away her tears. As she turned to go he handed her a carefully folded rectangle of paper, sealed with a blob of a red wax, which she slipped in to her coat pocket without inspection.

'My dear, you might have thought me unfeeling, but I am your father, and I know you have been suffering too these past few days. Trust in the Lord, my love, he has a way of making things come about.' He almost bundled her from the door, giving her no time to question his comment.

Jane was accompanying them and she was waiting patiently beside the open door of the carriage for Emma to climb in. It was the first of November and the wind was sharp, blowing her pelisse around her feet and causing her to grab on to the brim of her bonnet. She stepped nimbly up to join her sister, delighted to see fur rugs in which to wrap themselves and hot bricks upon which to place their feet.

The excitement of the journey made her forget about the letter her father had given her; she was as entranced as her sister at the scenes that passed by the windows. They stopped to change horses at the Red Lion in Colchester. She was very impressed that her grandparents could afford to have two sets of spare animals waiting for them en route to their palatial country estate in Richmond. However, as the day became dark and cold her enjoyment had long since turned into discomfort and boredom. They had drawn the blinds and conversation between them had all but ceased.

'How much longer is it going to be before we arrive, Emma?'

'I have no idea, as I have told you many times before, but I imagine it cannot be much further. When we stopped for supper an hour ago the coachman said we should be arriving at eight o'clock, and although I cannot see to check my chronometer, I'm sure it must be almost that by now.'

She heard her sister sigh loudly and shift about vigorously on the seat. The carriage rocked alarmingly and for a moment she feared it was Eugenie's antics that had caused them to bounce. One of the blinds rolled up of its own volition and she saw to her delight the vehicle had been turning in to a long driveway. The gatehouse stood to the left and flambeaux burned brightly on either side illuminating the magnificence of the wrought iron gates and the high redbrick wall that snaked off on either side into the darkness.

'Look, we're almost there. Quickly, Jane, whilst we have the light from the torches, help us to replace our bonnets and wipe the grime from our faces.'

The carriage appeared to travel for a further fifteen minutes before Emma could see any signs of the house they were to spend the next few months in. 'I see it! To our right, Eugenie, there's a blaze of lights. Good heavens! Such extravagance! I do believe they must have put candles in every window in the house to welcome us; and there appear to be a prodigious amount of windows.'

'Such an enormous building, and recently constructed I think. Can you see the columns flanking the front door, and there must be two dozen footmen standing on either side of the steps.' Eugenie flopped back, shaking her head in disbelief. 'I had no idea Mama came from such a wealthy family.'

Emma's mouth tightened. If they were so rich, why had they left their only daughter to pinch and scrape to make ends meet? She was disposed to dislike them already. 'It will be like living in an army barracks, the place is so huge.'

Her sister giggled. 'Without the hundreds of common soldiers, of course. You do say such peculiar things sometimes, Emma.'

The coach lurched to a halt, the door flung open and the steps down before Emma had time to reply. An arm was offered to help her alight, but she ignored it. She waited for her sister and Jane to descend then looked up, expecting to see her grandparents waiting to greet them at the head of the steps.

The two figures coming towards them were definitely not Sir James and Lady Masterson; one was an elderly man in black tail coat the other an elderly lady in navy bombazine. These must be the butler and housekeeper. Her heart dipped into her boots; if her grandparents could not be bothered to appear in person they were obviously not welcome. This was a duty visit, something to be endured by both sides and ended as soon as good manners allowed.

She paused, allowing her sister to draw up beside her and slipped her arm through hers. 'Smile politely, nod your head, but do not curtsy or be over familiar. These are superior servants and they will treat us abominably if we do not set the correct tone.' These words were spoken quietly so that even Jane could not overhear.

'Welcome to Singleton Manor, Miss Meadows, Miss Eugenie. I am Foster, and this is Mrs Truman, who will take care of you and conduct you to your apartment.'

Emma nodded regally and with Eugenie at her side swept past them as if she dealt with situations such as this every day of the week. Her heart was pounding and she felt unwelcome perspiration trickling down between her shoulder blades.

She didn't pause to admire the spacious marble-floored entrance hall with its galleried balcony and double sweeping staircase. Instead she continued her stately progress and began to ascend the one on the left. She heard the clatter of footsteps behind her and knew that the housekeeper had been forced to run in order to catch up with them.

Smiling in spite of her nervousness, Emma didn't halt until she reached the landing on the first floor. She risked a glance at her sister and saw her lips twitching and knew there was a grave danger of them both collapsing into unseemly giggles if they didn't reach the sanctuary of their chambers soon.

'I beg your pardon, madam, for being so tardy. If you would care to follow me I shall conduct you to the apartment Lady Masterson has chosen for you.'

Two footmen dodged past in order to open the double doors with a flourish. They bowed in synchronised servility and, as before, Emma ignored them. She swished into the rooms that she was to share with Eugenie for the next few weeks at least.

There were two immaculately dressed chambermaids standing to attention by the door. They dipped in matching curtsies and again Emma and Eugenie merely nodded. The housekeeper pointed to the first girl. 'This is Mary and that is her sister Beth; they shall be for your personal use during your stay here. I hope you find everything you need; please send one of the girls down if there is anything else you require.'

'Thank you, Mrs Truman. I'm sure that we have everything we need. However, if we don't I shall let you know at once.'

The woman backed out and the door closed behind her. Emma breathed a sigh of relief — she had hated acting the part of a supercilious mistress and was glad she could now return to her usual demeanour. She addressed the two girls who were shifting nervously from foot to foot.

'Jane is our personal maid, but she will be pleased to have your assistance. Perhaps, Mary, you could act as Miss Eugenie's abigail?' She had selected Mary, as she was obviously her sister's senior by several years.

The girl's face lit up. 'I should be honoured, madam. I love to sew, if you have any repairs or alterations I should be delighted to do them for you.'

'Then you are the perfect choice for me, Mary. Come, would you both show us around our new abode?'

Eugenie's enthusiasm was infectious and soon Emma was exclaiming as loudly as her sister over the luxurious appointments. They were to share a bed chamber but not a bed. The room was so vast that two beds could easily be accommodated and still leave room for pretty tables and a *chaise-longue* under the window.

'In here, Miss Meadows, you have a commodious dressing room with two large closets and many shelves and drawers.'

Emma exchanged a glance with her sister; the garments they had brought with them would scarcely fill a corner of the cupboard. Mary was unaware of their amusement and ran forward to open the door of yet another room. The girl stepped aside and waited for them to join her.

'My goodness! Emma, we have our very own bathing room. I have heard of such things but never thought to use one myself.'

The room was full of rose-perfumed steam and Emma gasped in delight. 'Eugenie, we have a bath full of hot water waiting for us. I never imagined such a luxury.'

A roaring coal fire filled the grate and

bath sheets were warming on the stands on either side.

'Mrs Truman thought that after your long journey you would enjoy a hot soak. If, Miss Meadows, you would care to step behind the screen, your Jane can assist you to disrobe.'

'No, Mary, thank you. You help Miss Eugenie into the bath, I shall wait my turn.'

She left her sister to enjoy the novel experience and retreated through the bed chamber and back to the pretty parlour that made up their suite of rooms. In their absence someone had come in and left a tray on the mahogany table standing just inside the door.

'Sit down, miss, by the fire and I shall bring you something to eat and drink,' Jane instructed.

'Whatever it is, it smells delicious. How thoughtful of someone to think of us like this.' She was demolishing her second plate of game pie and delicious chutney when Eugenie emerged, her cheeks flushed, looking totally relaxed.

'At last! I thought you drowned, you have been so long. I hope the water is still warm enough for me.'

'You are to have fresh water, Emma. Mary sent Beth down for it as soon as I got out. Do you know, she pulled out the stopper and the water vanished like magic. I could hear it gurgling down a pipe, I wonder where it goes.'

'I've no idea, my love. Come and sit by the fire and let Jane fetch you some of this delicious pie. I hadn't realised how famished I was until the plate was placed in front of me.' She called across to Jane who was busy serving up a portion of supper for the new arrival. 'What else is there? I have room for something else if it is as tasty as my first course.'

Well-fed and freshly bathed, Emma climbed into her bed which, she was touched to note, had been warmed. Eugenie was asleep seconds after she vanished beneath the comforter, but Emma could not settle. In spite of being warm and feeling more relaxed than she had in days, her thoughts kept turning to the man she had lost, wondering if he was feeling as wretched as she. The fact that her grandparents were away from home, indeed had left that very morning for a more pressing engagement and had not been present to greet them, did nothing to calm her overwrought sensibilities. Sir James and Lady Masterson had made it perfectly clear how matters stood between them. Eugenie and herself might be blood relatives but they were obviously not considered to be of any great importance; they had been abandoned to the care of servants, to sink or swim as they would. She fell asleep as the clock in the sitting-room struck midnight, her pillow sodden, not knowing how she could face the next few days with equanimity.

8

Emma woke at dawn and, finding her sister still asleep, slipped on her robe and went into the sitting-room where she found an unknown maidservant on her knees in front of the grate, cleaning it out in preparation for another fire. The girl jumped nervously and started to scramble up, scattering ash on the carpet.

'Please don't get up; here, let me help you.' Before the girl could protest Emma tied her robe more securely and dropped to her knees. Taking the copper pan and matching brush she quickly swept away the mess.

'Thank you, Miss Meadows. I'm that sorry, but Mrs Truman said as I was to not wake you, but to make sure you had a lovely big fire going when you came in here this morning.'

'You didn't wake me, I'm an early

riser; it was very kind of Mrs Truman to think of us.' Emma stood up. 'What's your name? I should like to be able to address you correctly if you're to be here every morning.'

'It's Lilly, miss.'

'Well, Lilly, I shall leave you to your duties. I'm going to sit on the window seat and look out on to the park, it was too dark to see anything when we arrived last night.'

She deliberately didn't ask for any refreshments to be sent for. Jane would take care of that herself, and it was important that their abigail made herself known below stairs as soon as possible. Also Jane might well discover the whereabouts of her grandparents, something she hadn't liked to enquire about, as gossiping with servants was not done.

Soon the room was warm and Lilly had vanished through a door in the wall. She relaxed and gazed out across the rolling parkland. There was something vaguely familiar about the vista and she smiled at the recollection that it was an exact facsimile of a plate she'd seen in a copy of Ackerman's Repository. The grounds, she was sure, had been landscaped by no other than Capability Brown. It had been made to look like something out of a picture, there was even a manufactured Greek temple placed on a convenient slope in the distance. The ornamental lake was dull and grey in the early morning light; she noticed that the sky was heavy, and feared it was going to rain before luncheon. Raining or not, she was determined to go outside and explore. It was her first time away from home and although she had not wished to come, now she was here she intended to make the most of it; she might never have another opportunity.

Stealthily she re-entered her bed chamber and tiptoed across the wide expanse of floral carpet to enter the dressing room; she came face-to-face with Mary, who was, at that very moment laying out her walking dress, the necessary under garments, a warm cloak, gloves and bonnet.

The girl dipped and smiled. 'Good morning, Miss Meadows. Lilly said that you was already awake, so I came up at once to put out your clothes. Miss Jane is assembling your breakfast tray and will have it up here by the time you're ready.' With such deft fingers to help her Emma was soon dressed. Still wearing her indoor slippers, she sat in the parlour, her sister undisturbed.

Jane greeted her cheerily. 'I have chocolate here, miss, and as Cook has just baked, I've brought you up some fresh rolls and some of her preserve.'

'Thank you. I intend to go outside and have a look around, and this will fortify me beautifully. Did you discover when breakfast is served here?'

'It seems it will be served whenever you and Miss Eugenie wish it to be. I said that nine o'clock would suit, I hope that's right?'

'Exactly, for I doubt that Miss Eugenie will be awake and ready before then.' How accommodating the staff were here, and to think she had thought them unfriendly when she had arrived. The distance had been on her side, not theirs. 'Jane, could you bear to come with me? If I'm to get lost, I'd sooner do it in company.'

Jane grinned, flicking aside the skirt of her plain blue dress, revealing she was already wearing stout boots. 'I only have to run upstairs and get my cloak and bonnet and I'm ready.'

Fifteen minutes later Emma was leaving her rooms, warmly dressed and eager to explore. To her astonishment there was a footman waiting outside her door. He jumped to attention and bowed.

'Good morning, Miss Meadows. Mr Foster said I was to be your guide until you are familiar with the house.'

'How thoughtful of him, thank you. Tell me, what am I to call you?'

The young man bowed again. 'I'm Jonathan, and I shall be at your service at all times.'

'Thank you, Jonathan. I must own that I am relieved to see you. I had visions of myself and my abigail wandering lost in this huge establishment for weeks.'

Her escort grinned, revealing him to be far younger than she thought, little more than a youth, really.

'I reckon you'll soon get used to it, Miss Meadows. Mr Foster has said as we're all to keep an eye out for you, make sure you don't feel uncomfortable.'

She followed him down the wide passageway, noting there were several similar doors on either side which were obviously other bed chambers. They emerged on the wide gallery that overlooked the massive, marble-floored entrance hall she had been so impressed with the night before. She ran forward to lean on the polished oak balustrade, staring down with pleasure at the space below.

'Look at this, Jane, it's magnificent. The ceiling must be at least sixty feet

— and see these wonderful mouldings, we could be in a palace, not a domestic dwelling.' Her maid was hanging back nervously and Emma remembered the girl disliked heights. 'Never mind, let's descend. I wish to go outside and have a look round before the rain comes. Eugenie and I can explore indoors later today.'

Foster appeared and bowed formally. 'Good morning, Miss Meadows. I trust that you slept well. I have arranged for Jonathan to be your guide this morning, and for as long as you need him. He has been here three years and is quite capable of taking you anywhere you wish to go.'

Emma eyed the young man. He was dressed smartly in bottle green livery, but it was his indoor garb, and she doubted Foster would allow him to fetch a cloak. She couldn't refuse, but was determined to send the boy back as soon as she could.

'Thank you, Foster.' Belatedly, she remembered Mama had said that you never thanked a servant, they were merely doing their duty, what they were paid for. It had always seemed impolite to her.

She turned to Jonathan, who was hovering anxiously beside her, unsettled by the presence of the austere butler. 'I should like to go the stables, I think. I love horses, although in the last few years I have had little contact with them.'

'In that case, Miss Meadows, we had best go out by the side door. There's a path that leads directly from there, it's the one Sir James uses.'

He led them across the hall, their boots clicking noisily on the marble, down a wide passageway, and around a corner and then the floor was carpeted again, her boots quiet. Eventually the young man stopped, opening a door on to a gravel path that led, straight as an arrow, through a naked archway of wisteria. Its black branches were empty of foliage and flowers, but it would look stunning in the early summer. She wondered if she would be here to see it bloom.

The stables were a short distance from the house and the brisk walk brought much-needed colour to her cheeks; she could hear the welcome clatter of buckets and hooves, the occasional whinny and the laughing shouts of the grooms as they worked. It was only eight o'clock, but already everyone was up and busy, apparently happy to be so. Papa had told her one could tell a lot from the condition and demeanour of the staff; if they were well fed, smartly dressed and content, then their masters would be good people too.

Jane had informed her the reason her grandparents had left unexpectedly was to attend the birth of the third child of Uncle Patrick and his wife, Eleanor Masterson. Emma quite understood their desire to be present, especially as the arrival of the baby was premature, but to leave without a note of any sort did show a lack of feeling that bothered her.

She was beginning to revise her initial impressions of both the house and its owners because everyone she had met had been so accommodating. All were going out of their way to make sure she was content, and these instructions could only have been given by her grandparents. The apartments they had been allocated were sumptuously appointed, everything of the best quality, and they had not one, but two personal maids to take care of them.

There was no further time for introspection as Jonathan led her round the corner of the huge, grey stone building and through an archway into an immaculate cobbled stable yard. Emma's eyes widened. Why there must be more than two dozen loose boxes, three quarters of them with eager equine heads poking out, all with burnished manes and shining eyes.

As well as heights, Jane also disliked horses, so Emma didn't ask her to do more than stand and wait in the shelter of the archway. 'I shall not be that long,

Jane, and if you get cold, feel free to return to the house. I shall have no difficulty finding my way back. Jonathan, you may return, I'm sure you have other duties to perform.'

A tidily-dressed man of middle years and florid complexion, wearing a bottle green jacket, waistcoat and smart blue neckerchief, approached her, a smile of welcome on his face.

'Good morning, Miss Meadows, you're most welcome. I see that you're not dressed for riding; have you come to select a mount for yourself? We have several beasts suitable for ladies.'

'I'm afraid that I'm a novice rider, but am hoping that Sir James will arrange for me to have instruction.'

Sam Roberts, the head groom introduced her to all the horses, both riding and carriage. He explained that the empty boxes, twelve of them, were for the horses that were accompanying her grandparents. Good heavens! It cost more to keep a single groom and horse than it did a house full of indoor servants — she could hardly imagine the wealth in this establishment if they could afford to keep so many animals.

'We've seen all the horses now, miss, have you taken a fancy to any of them?'

'I think that Silver Star is very pretty; Miss Eugenie, I believe will settle for her.' She turned to survey the boxes again. All the horses were handsome, but none of them had especially appealed to her. Just then, a loud banging and kicking coming from the far corner of the yard, from a box that was closed, attracted her attention.

'What animal do you have incarcerated in there? Why is his box closed?'

Sam shook his head. 'It's a new gelding Sir James purchased before he left; it's a wild one, will let no one in, takes a lump out of all the grooms who see to him. I expect the master will sell him on, he doesn't like bad temperament in his animals.'

'I should like to see him. It's possible he's merely upset and the strangeness of his new surroundings is making him behave out of character.'

Not waiting for a refusal — after all, she was the mistress here in the absence of her grandmother — she walked briskly to the box and stood, tapping her foot to show her determination to enter. Roberts reluctantly slid back the bolts. The door swung back, but no angry head shot forward with gnashing teeth. Surprised, Emma peered into the darkness and saw a huge horse standing pressed against the manger, his ears back, his eyes rolling, not in anger but in fear.

Without hesitation she unlatched the lower door and walked in, speaking softly to the terrified animal. 'There, boy, no one is going to hurt you. I know just how you feel. It's hateful to be removed from familiar surroundings, to hear only strange voices. Look, I shall be your friend.'

Emma made no attempt to touch him; she knew enough about animals to understand she risked being bitten if she startled him. She stood still, not looking directly at him, and then turned her back, appearing disinterested. Sam and another groom remained poised anxiously in the doorway, ready to come to her assistance if necessary.

There was a faint snuffling behind her and then she felt a gentle nudge on her shoulder. She ignored it and continued to stare ahead, as if there was something of great interest at the far side of the box. A second nudge, and an enormous chestnut head was gently lowered over her shoulder and a whiskery muzzle began breathing gently on to her shoulder. Now was the time to make physical contact. Slowly, so as not to alarm him, she raised her hand and rested it on his cheek, scratching behind his ear gently, then she put her other arm around his nose and embraced him. Slowly she turned to face the massive beast, still not making eye contact, and rested her face against his.

For a few moments they breathed in unison, and Emma felt the horse relax.

This was the horse she wanted to learn to ride on. He was too big and too high-spirited for a novice, but as soon as she had seen his coat was exactly the same shade of red as her hair, her heart was touched and she knew she would settle for no other.

Reaching up she grasped the length of rope dangling beneath his halter and led him outside. 'Come along then. I shall take you around and introduce you to the other members of this yard.' The horse ambled along behind her to the astonishment of all the grooms he had been terrorizing.

Sam Roberts was standing by the door scratching his head, grinning widely. 'Never seen the like, all he needed was a bit of love. I thought I knew horses, but I got it wrong with this fellow. His name is Firebrand, by the way, Miss.'

Firebrand. It was an excellent name and suited the horse perfectly. Emma spent a contented half hour leading her new friend around the yard, and by the time he returned to his stable he was no longer a danger to himself or others.

It was a simple route to the house and she found her way to the side door with no difficulty, but when she was inside she wasn't sure in which direction to go. As she hesitated, Jonathan sped round the corner, his wig askew, and skidded to a halt in front of her.

'There, a stable lad raced down to the kitchen with a message that you were on your way back. I'm sorry if I kept you waiting, Miss Meadows, it's a long way round to the side door.'

Upstairs, Eugenie was disappointed she'd missed the excursion to the stables. 'You should have waited for me, Emma, and now it's raining.'

'I'm going to wash and change, then we can go down to breakfast together; we have the inside of the house to explore and we have our very own footman to help us do so.'

Not only was there a breakfast room, but also a small dining-room as well as the grand chamber used when company was present. The housekeeper came in to see them whilst they were eating breakfast to discover their wishes for the day. Emma was quick to tell Mrs Truman that they required no more than soup, or bread and cheese at midday, that they did not take afternoon tea, and would have a simple repast in the evening served in the small dining-room without fuss.

With so much to occupy her, Emma scarcely had time to miss her father or wonder about the continued absence of their grandparents. Being busy also helped a little to alleviate the loss of Lord Denver. She had discovered that there was a library running the length of the house, the front wall broken by dozens of windows, the rear wall with floor-to-ceiling shelves all filled with handsome leather-bound books of every description. Eugenie had fallen with delight upon a dozen of the latest novels, and exclaimed with joy at the books of fashion plates and ladies' magazines. Emma discovered a volume which gave detailed instructions on learning to ride. Admittedly it was aimed at gentlemen, but there was one chapter on the use of the side saddle. She had returned three times to the stables and been shown how to lunge Firebrand in the indoor school, but without a riding habit could not begin her lessons.

When Emma had discussed the events of that fateful night with her sister she was relieved to discover Eugenie no longer blamed Denver, indeed, said that he had done everything he should, the fault was all his brother's, and as long as she never saw *him* again, she would not hold a grudge against his lordship. It was decided that when Emma wrote to her father at the weekend she would enclose a note for Lord Denver saying how sorry she was that she had been unable to speak to him and that she would be more than ready to see him when she returned in the New Year. She prayed that he might have returned to Kesgrave Abbey by then.

On Saturday morning the girls decided to walk across the park because Eugenie wished to investigate the folly at the far side of the lake. Jane had laid out her outdoor garments before leaving to don her own cloak. This was the first occasion Emma had worn this pelisse since she had arrived earlier in the week. She felt the rustle of paper in her pocket and pulled out the letter her father had given her. She had quite forgotten about it. She had not written to him yet, and felt it would not be politic to tell him that her grandparents were absent, but had decided she would write as soon as they returned which, according to Mary, was to be that very day.

She turned the letter over and saw the bold black writing. This was not from her father; it was a scrawl she had seen once before, written on her dance card. This was a letter from Lord Denver. He must have composed it when he had visited last Saturday but Papa, for some reason had not given it to her until she had left on the Wednesday. Why had she not thought to check in her pocket until now?

Smoothing out the paper she scanned the contents. Her cry of anguish echoed around the parlour and she collapsed, shaking, on to a convenient chair.

9

Relieved that she was alone, Emma held the paper in shaking fingers and read it for a second time.

My dear Miss Meadows,
I fully understand your reasons for not speaking to me this morning and so am writing this letter to you to explain my actions last night and this morning.
I was forced to leave you alone on the dance floor because my brother took your sister away and I feared for her safety. I was right to do so, as his intentions were not honourable. I arrived in time and sent Miss Eugenie home in the carriage which is why you were obliged to wait.
My brother will be leaving Kesgrave Abbey for ever as soon as I return from here. I am sending him to

*India. He must learn to be respon-
sible and repent his actions before he
may return and be accepted as my
brother.*

*I shall be away for three days; I shall
see him on to the ship myself and
make sure that he stays there. Then I
shall return here for the answer to
this question. My dear Miss Meadows, I have come to regard you with
the deepest affection over the past
few weeks and am praying that you
reciprocate my feelings.*

*If there is no letter waiting for me
then I shall know you want none of
me. I shall follow my brother to
India and you have my word as a
gentleman that I shall not live in
Kesgrave Abbey whilst you or your
sister are still in residence at the vicarage.*

*I remain yours in love and expec-
tation,*
Richard Tennent.

If only Papa had given her the letter as

he should have, if only she had read it straight away, then there would still have been time to send a reply. Now it was too late. Richard, for he had become that in her heart, would have departed for India thinking she had rejected him.

She had never felt such pain. Even when Mama had died she had not felt so devastated — but then, her mother had always been a rather distant figure in her life. Aggie and Papa had supplied the love and affection she and Eugenie needed.

A sob escaped through her clenched teeth and she rocked in misery, the letter from her beloved crushed against her heart.

'Emma, my love, whatever's wrong?'

Too overcome to answer she held out the mangled letter and felt it removed from her fingers. Then a soft cloth was placed in her fingers and obediently she mopped her eyes and blew her nose loudly.

'It might not be too late. You should

write immediately. Lord Denver will have left Papa a forwarding address at the very least. Your missive can be sent on if necessary, and you can be certain he will return immediately when he realises what has happened.'

'You're right. I am giving way to despair and not thinking things through.' Her sister's sensible solution had begun to calm her and she was able to think rationally once more. Of course she should send a letter after Richard; he loved her as she loved him and would come back as soon as he received the news.

'I shall write immediately. If we send a footman he can give it directly to the mail coach. It should be in Kesgrave by tomorrow morning.' She swallowed. It was the Sabbath day and no letters would be delivered until Monday.

Her letter was sealed and Eugenie ran downstairs to find Foster. They had decided he would be the best person to deal with the emergency. Emma still had on her outdoor coat and walking boots, but she didn't feel like trekking across the park any more.

'Jane, I shall remain here after all.' She sat down on the window seat and let her abigail remove her boots, something she normally did for herself. Then she held out each arm passively whilst her pelisse was removed. She heard the sound of voices approaching rapidly along the corridor outside and before she could retreat into the privacy of her bedchamber, the door burst open and what could only be her grandmother erupted into the parlour.

'Oh my dear, the letter, I do apologise, how stupid of me! I said to dear James, did I not, my love? How could I be so dunderheaded as to forget it? What must you think of us, abandoning you without a word? Come here, my love, and let me embrace you.' Lady Masterson held out her arms and when Emma remained rooted to the spot she ran forward and grasped her warmly. 'I cannot tell you how much I have been longing for this moment.

Although we now have another grand-daughter, you and Eugenie are the daughters of my firstborn and so especially dear to us, are they not, Sir James?'

Emma was drowning under a deluge of words, hardly able to understand what was being said. How could her grandmother know about the letter? It was too much and she felt a strange light-headedness and the chatter faded mercifully into darkness.

★　★　★

'Here, Emma, sip this lemonade, it is cool and will restore you.'

She was in her bedroom, stretched out on the comforter, with Eugenie and Jane hovering anxiously at her side. Of her loquacious grandmother there was no sign, for which she was heartily thankful.

'I have never fainted in my life before; but it was too much — having them arrive so suddenly when I was feeling so distracted.'

'Poor, Emma, I don't blame you for having a fit of the vapours. For a tiny woman our revered grandparent produces a deal of noise. But it was not your letter she was referring to. It seems she wrote a note to us explaining where they'd gone and then took it with her by mistake.'

Eugenie removed the cup from her lips and laughed. 'She *is* very talkative, but so kind. She was devastated when you fainted, and when Grandfather took her away she was in floods of tears and blaming herself.'

'I shall go and speak to her right away. They must think me a poor specimen after my performance.' She swung her feet to the floor and was relieved to find no residual dizziness. 'Shall you come with me, Eugenie? Oh, did you manage to send my letter before our grandparents arrived?'

'Yes and yes. Here, let me help you with your hair, you look like a fiery Medusa at the moment.'

Jonathan was once more on duty outside the door. Foster had been shocked that one of *his* young ladies had been obliged to run through the house with an urgent message. In future, Eugenie explained to Emma as they strolled arm in arm behind him, he was to wait outside the door just in case he was needed.

They were conducted to the main drawing-room, a room they had not used before. It had seemed presumptuous to sit there in the absence of their host and hostess. Emma thought the room overdone. Her grandmother had adopted the Egyptian style and everywhere the furniture legs had the appearance of clawed feet and an overabundance of gilt work. However, it was warm and welcoming, as were her two relatives.

This time it was Sir James who took the lead; her grandmother was sitting, subdued and sad, upon a chair. Emma curtsied to her grandfather and then hurried over to drop to her knees beside

Lady Masterson.

'I am so sorry that our first meeting ended in disarray. I have been so looking forward to it, but I had just received such distressing news and became confused.'

Lady Masterson took her hands and squeezed them fondly. 'It is I that owe you an apology. I rattle on so and forget that others find it disagreeable. I shall try and be quieter whilst you are both with us.'

'You must do no such thing, Grandmamma, this is your home and you must behave exactly as you always do, it is I who must become more agreeable.' Smiling she rose gracefully and took the seat adjacent. 'I should like to tell you both what happened, but before I do that please tell me about my new cousin. Is Aunt Marianne in good health?'

'Indeed she is, my dear girl. And the little baby, so sweet, so adorable . . . ' A faint cough from Sir James made her pause. 'They are coming to visit for the

Christmas season and I can tell you that your Uncle Patrick is beside himself in his eagerness to meet you both. Do you know we had no idea of your existence until your father sent us the sad tidings of our dear Lydia's demise.'

Her grandfather, as tall and thin as her grandmother was small and round, folded his length on to an opposite armchair, crossed his legs at the ankle and beamed at her. 'Much as we loved our daughter, she was more like her grandfather than either of us.' He stopped. 'More of this later. Now, I should like to hear what had distressed you so, my dear?'

Emma quickly told them the whole sorry story, making sure that Eugenie appeared an innocent party, and they were instantly sympathetic. Sir James surged to his feet.

'And the name of your young man is Richard Tennent, now Lord Denver?'

'It is. He was a major with the Duke of Wellington, but I have no idea which regiment he was in.'

'Lord Denver? Sounds familiar. Let me think . . . Yes, I remember now, his uncle was also an investor in the shipping line that I am involved with. It will be with them that Denver will travel. I shall send word immediately to their head office in London and make sure that he's waylaid before he sails. You're lucky, my dear, there are storms in the Channel at the moment and no ships are sailing so it is unlikely that Denver will have embarked for India.'

Emma couldn't believe it. Her emotions were in turmoil — she was normally such an even-tempered young woman and now she felt herself buffeted by events and was having difficulty understanding if she was elated or dejected.

'Go at once, send your letter post-haste, Sir James. I shall not have my darling girl so unhappy whilst we can do something to help.'

He strode from the room leaving the three ladies together to catch up on each other's lives and hear more about the new cousin, to be called Emma Eugenie. It seemed that her family was overjoyed to find they had more members to add to it. Her grandmother also explained that Sir James senior, now happily defunct, had demanded immediate and absolute obedience from all members of his family. Although he had been given his baronetcy for services to the Crown, which simply meant he had lent them money at an attractive rate, he had believed that his granddaughter was good enough to marry into the true aristocracy, and had threatened to disown Sir James if he gave his permission for the marriage of his daughter to their papa.

'He had no choice, my dears, Lydia was determined to go her own way. She waited until she was one and twenty and then left here and we never spoke to her again. Your father was a curate at the church in the next parish before he received the living he has now in

Kesgrave, but they vanished without telling us where they had gone.'

'Grandmamma, it is in the past. We are here now and have no intention of being strangers to you ever again. When we return home in the New Year it will be in the firm expectation of being invited to visit again in the spring.'

'Return in the New Year? I hope you do not intend to leave before next summer, Emma my dear. We are planning to give you a season in Town, indeed I have already booked the orchestra for your ball to be held in April. I never had the chance to launch my daughter into society and fully intend to do for you that which I could never do for her.'

'A season? Emma, do you hear that? We shall go to balls and soirées, routs and parties and meet new people and see new things.'

At the mention of so much frivolity Emma's heart sunk. 'Forgive me, Grandmamma, but I cannot leave Papa alone to go gallivanting around in

London. Eugenie must stay, she loves to dance and socialise, but I prefer a quiet life and would hate it.' She expected a barrage of persuasion but Lady Masterson smiled lovingly at her.

'You shall do exactly as you wish, my love. I know just how you feel, Sir James is dreading it too, but is prepared to endure for my sake. Family parties are quite different though, and I'm sure you will enjoy the festivities I have planned for you here.'

The rest of the day passed in happy conversation and when Emma retired to her room, pleading a headache after her upset earlier, she left Eugenie happily exchanging ideas and schemes with her grandmother. Her head was reeling, and she needed peace and quiet, to be on her own for a while. She had so much to think about, not least that Sir James had settled 30,000 guineas on each of them, to be theirs without restriction on their marriage or on attaining five and twenty. She would be that age on her next name day, March the first.

Jane was nowhere to be seen, and their apartments were blessedly quiet. Even Jonathan had gone about other business, believing her in the drawing-room with her grandparents. Sir James had set things in motion and assured her that no expense would be spared in fetching Richard to her side. She smiled when she imagined his reaction to being summoned to Singleton Manor. He wouldn't have had her letter and as far as she knew he was unaware that Sir James Masterson was a relative of hers.

Well, there was nothing she could do about it now. If he came in high dudgeon then she could soon smooth his ruffled feathers and make all well between them. She settled back on the window seat and let her imagination free. They could be married in Kes-grave Church by her father, in the spring when the daffodils were in full bloom.

In the vicarage all was not well. 'Are you telling me, sir, that you neglected to hand my urgent letter to your daughter until she left on Wednesday?' Richard could scarcely contain his fury. He was not used to having his instructions ignored. When he had written the letter he had supposed Emma would read it the same day and write him a reply, or ignore him, and he would know exactly how he stood.

'I beg your pardon, Lord Denver, but what with one thing and another and my pastoral duties, it quite slipped my mind. If you had told me the contents at the time then this misunderstanding would not have taken place.'

He felt his anger drain away. Mr Meadows was quite correct. In fact, he should never have written such a letter without first speaking to him about his intentions. He smiled and held out his hand. 'I apologise for my outburst. I have no right to speak to you in that way. Indeed, as I'm hoping that you will become my father-in-law very soon, it was a remarkably stupid thing to do.'

The older man laughed at his discomfiture. 'Forget it, my dear boy. You have my blessing, and although Emma did not reply I believe, in fact I'm certain, that she returns your feelings. I cannot understand why she hasn't written to you, I do hope nothing untoward has happened on the journey?'

Richard stared at him. 'You do not even know if they arrived safely in Richmond?'

Mr Meadows shook his head. 'Don't look so anxious, bad news always travels fast. If they had met with a mishap I would certainly have heard about it. No, for some reason Emma has not written to us, but I'm sure it is not because either she or Eugenie have met with a disaster.'

'I shall ride there directly. If I travel post I could be there first thing tomorrow morning.' He frowned — tomorrow was Sunday; it would not do to arrive unannounced on the Sabbath.

'My daughter will not be going anywhere, my boy, so I should take your time. Travel in your own carriage in comfort, overnight in Colchester and Romford, arrive rested and relaxed on Monday, not in a pelter tomorrow. Or why not leave it until Monday, there's no hurry after all.'

'Excellent advice. In fact, I think I shall find myself lodgings in the vicinity and send word to Sir James and Lady Masterson before arriving on their doorstep unannounced. As you have so sensibly pointed out, sir, it makes little difference if I arrive in one day or five, as long as I do arrive.'

★   ★   ★

So it was that whilst he was driving to Richmond, Emma's letter was flying to Kesgrave and Sir James had organised for a dozen or more of his employees to begin searching the docks for him. As far as Richard was concerned he was riding to claim the woman he loved, believing there was no urgency, whilst Emma as the days passed, became more agitated, believing that he'd already left the country and was lost to her . . .

10

On Monday the skies were clear and although a trifle chilly it was a perfect morning for Eugenie and Emma to begin their riding lessons. They had each received a riding habit as a welcome gift from their grandparents. These had been bought ready-made but fortunately needed little alteration.

'The military style is the height of fashion, Emma, and this will be the first time we've ever dressed in matching outfits. This deep blue is perfect for both of us, but I believe the cap is better suited to your oval face than it is to mine.'

'We both look splendid. Roberts is to take our lesson. Grandpapa has promised not to come and watch until we are more confident. I'm surprised he didn't question our choice of mounts as I know that Firebrand is totally unsuitable for a novice, especially a female one.'

Gathering up her gloves and whip she was ready to leave. She prayed that the huge chestnut was as eager to carry her as she was to ride him; it was a long way to fall if he decided he didn't like her on board.

The lesson went better than she could have expected, neither of them had recourse to leading reins and they were both able to walk, trot and canter safely by the end of the two hours.

'I'm stiff and sore after so long in the saddle,' Eugenie complained as they retraced their steps to their apartment. 'I don't remember riding being so uncomfortable.'

'As neither of us has done so for over ten years, and then never off the leading rein, I don't think we have anything to compare it with. Mary promised we should have a hot bath when we returned, and as you are so stiff you may go first. I shall write again to Papa, I have yet to tell him how delightful our grandparents have turned out to be, or the real reason they did not contact us until five years ago.'

'I should think Lord Denver might have received your letter today if he was still in Kesgrave, so he might arrive tomorrow or the next day.'

'I'm trying not to think about it, Eugenie, so please don't keep reminding me of what *might* be as it is quite possible he has already sailed for India. Grandpapa said yesterday that he would go to London himself if we hear nothing tomorrow.'

The next two days were spent with riding lessons in the morning, and morning calls in the afternoon. Emma found it strange that in society the morning ran from midday until four o'clock. She understood it to be because most hostesses didn't rise until late morning as they had been attending parties until the small hours.

They had met many of the local gentry and already her sister had two gentlemen callers. It was as if Mr

Tennent had never existed. She resigned herself to the fact that it was going to be a long winter, with her sister falling in and out of love with every new beau that called bringing posies and dreadful poems for her delectation.

Thursday came and went with still no word from Kesgrave or London about the whereabouts of her missing suitor. Sir James returned with nothing good to report; as far as he could ascertain no one of the name of Tennent or Denver had left for India in the last month.

'Could this mean that Lord Denver was deliberately misleading me about sending his brother abroad?' she asked her grandfather on Friday morning as they sat together eating breakfast.

'It could be. Perhaps the villain has just returned to Oxford and is carrying on his philandering. I shall send word there to see if he has appeared at his lodgings.' He shook his head sadly. 'However, my dear girl, I fear it will be a wild goose chase. The two of them have gone to ground somewhere, and all we can do is wait and see if Denver reappears.'

'Are you coming out with me this morning, Grandpapa? I cannot wait to take Firebrand for a proper excursion; we're both becoming bored with cantering around the indoor school and the paddock.'

'I'm sorry, my dear, but I have to meet my agent this morning. I promise that I shall come out with you tomorrow.'

At the stables her mount was ready and waiting, but of Sam Robertson there was no sign.

'Am I to ride alone this morning?'

The groom who had just tossed into the saddle nodded apologetically. 'Mr Roberts has had to go out this morning, but he said he would be back shortly and, if you don't mind, to practice in the paddock until he returns.'

'Very well. I can manage from here. I noticed that the paddock gate has been left open for me. I shall not detain you longer.' The young man looked as though he wished to argue but she dismissed him with a wave of her hand and he didn't dare disobey.

Waiting until he had vanished around the corner, Emma gathered up the reins and patted Firebrand's gleaming neck. 'We shall go out for a quiet hack around the park, we can come to no harm on our own and I'm sure that you're as bored as I being confined to the paddock and school these past few days.' Eugenie had, as was often the case, lost interest in riding after her first few lessons. She much preferred to sit and discuss her future wardrobe with Lady Masterson, which meant no-one else need know of Emma's foolhardiness.

The horse shook his head, his bit jangling loudly, but his ears were forward and he felt calm and relaxed beneath her. She knew she should wait until she was accompanied — although she had walked around the park it was still basically unknown to her and she had little idea which way would be the best for a beginner on what could be considered a highly unsuitable horse. Nonetheless, she clicked her tongue, lowered her hands and touched his flank with her heel and he moved smoothly off into a long easy walk. It was only as she left the gravel drive for the wide, leafy path that led into the woods that she realised the horse had not been out anywhere since his arrival. He was as ignorant of their surroundings as she was.

His hooves made no sound on the damp earth and the watery sun filtered through the bare branches, warming them both a little. The path widened and ran straight ahead for half a mile, ideal for her first trot of the day. Firebrand responded calmly to her instructions and they trotted in perfect harmony to the end of the path. At no time had he tried to pull away from her, to shy or behave in a way likely to unseat her. 'Good boy! I knew we should be fine together, I have no idea where to go now, so I shall let you choose.'

The path branched, the left-hand fork leading deeper into the wood, towards what looked like an open field above which she could see a distant church spire. Emma was relieved when her horse chose the fields, she believed she was less likely to get lost that way. She pushed him into a canter and he responded eagerly; this time she could feel his excitement, feel the power beneath her and knew that she was in danger of losing control completely. Deliberately she relaxed her hands and spoke soothingly to him and he settled down and carried her towards the gap. It was only as she got closer that she saw she would have to jump a ditch in order to reach the field.

She had no experience of jumping, her lessons had not reached that level. She was about to rein back when Firebrand took the decision from her hands and lengthening his stride headed at an extended canter for the obstacle. She was tempted to close her eyes and pray, but that would be the worst possible option. Instead she sat deep in to the saddle, wrapped her hands in his flying mane, and prayed they would not part company.

For a glorious moment she felt as though she was flying as she glanced down and saw the ditch vanish beneath them. Her horse landed without hesitation, but instead of slowing he extended his stride into a full gallop. All she could do was hang on and hope that he ran out of energy at the end of the field. She knew he was not bolting, that he would stop if she could regain her balance and pull hard on the reins as a more experienced rider would do, and that she was safe enough as long as she sat deep in her saddle and didn't panic.

All might still have been well if, at that precise moment, a rider on a magnificent black stallion had not appeared from a gap in the hedge directly into their path. Firebrand did exactly as he should — he swerved sideways, avoiding a collision that could have killed them both. However Emma's precarious balance was not sufficient to keep her in the saddle and she felt herself sailing into the air to land, with a painful thump, on her back in the mud.

★ ★ ★

The Green Man was an excellent establishment in every way, Richard thought, as he dropped his napkin on the empty plate. He had a clean, commodious bedchamber, his own private parlour in which he was now sitting, and they had excellent stabling facilities so he knew his horses were being well cared for.

It was Friday, and Enderby should be back from delivering his letter to Emma telling her he intended to call at three o'clock that afternoon. He had taken his future father-in-law's good advice and spent a leisurely three days travelling to Richmond, not starting his journey until Monday morning, like others not wishing to travel on Sunday if they could avoid it.

Black Knight, his stallion, would have recovered from the journey and would be as desperate as he to get out and stretch his legs in the bright November sunshine. He glanced at the mantel clock and saw it was a little after ten. He had plenty of time for a ride before coming back to change and be driven in his carriage to Singleton Manor.

He found Mitchell in the yard, cleaning harnesses alongside the coachman and groom who had also accompanied him to Richmond.

'Good morning, my lord, I can have Black Knight saddled and ready for you in a trice. He's itching to get out, and the ostler told me if you take the track down beside the church it will lead eventually through a hedge and into an open field where you can have a good gallop.'

'Excellent. Make sure Enderby

orders me a bath, and you make sure the carriage is spotless and the horses looking their best.'

He clattered out of the yard feeling the power beneath him, knowing that his horse would take hold of the bit with a lesser rider aboard. He sat back in the saddle and softened his hands and the horse responded immediately. They knew each other well, had spent several years riding across Spain and France and been involved in more than one skirmish together.

There! Up ahead he could finally see the tall hawthorn hedge he had been told about, and somewhere there would be a gap he could go through. He had been riding a few moments when he spotted it, he urged his horse forward into a trot and shot through the space. He heard the sound of galloping hooves and hauled back on the reins, forcing his horse back on his haunches, getting himself thoroughly entangled in the thorn-covered hedge.

He knew that his actions would have

been too little too late if the huge chestnut gelding had not taken evasive action as well; he also knew that the other rider had been flung from the saddle. Travelling at such speed he hated to think what damage might have been done to him.

It took him several minutes to disentangle himself from the hedge and vault from his saddle. He tossed the reins over the animal's head, knowing he would stay put. He stepped back into the field his face ashen, expecting to see a body spread-eagled before him. What he saw was the chestnut standing quietly, ears pricked, and the young woman he had come all this way to propose to, striding towards him incandescent with fury.

He was stupefied. What was she doing riding that horse? She had no more sense than her sister. Unfortunately he didn't have the wit to keep his thoughts to himself.

★　★　★

Emma sat up glad she had suffered no more harm than being winded and covered in mud. She saw Firebrand trotting back towards her with what could only be described as an anxious look on his face. In spite of her discomfort, and her growing fury at the idiot who had almost killed them, she smiled and held out her hand to the horse. He nuzzled it and then, as if understanding her dilemma, swung his huge bulk sideways so that she could grasp the single stirrup leather and pull herself upright. Her beautiful new habit was quite ruined, which added fuel to her anger. She slipped the reins over Firebrand's ears and looped them around her arm. She didn't think he would wander off, but she wanted to be sure.

Stepping round she faced for the first time the nincompoop that had caused the accident. Her mouth fell open and she gulped, swallowing a large amount of mud, which did nothing to improve her temper. Spitting dirt she approached him, eyes blazing, prepared to give him a piece of her mind. She had thought him lost to her, had spent the last few nights crying into her pillow, and here he was — not in India at all, and staring at her as if she was an inmate of Bedlam. The overwhelming relief that she had not lost him, combined with her justifiable ire was an explosive combination. She opened her mouth to berate him but he forestalled her.

'God's teeth, Emma. Have you run totally mad? First your sister shows as much sense as a pea-goose by believing every word Percy tells her, and now you attempt to kill us both by riding a totally unsuitable horse.'

How dare *he* accuse *her*? Her fragile self-control deserted her completely and she ran at him.

'You are a monster, and so is your brother! You dare to accuse *me* of having no sense? You nearly killed us both by your stupidity.' By the end of her tirade she was screaming, totally out of control. She hit him with a clenched fist directly in his left eye. An open handed slap would have been sufficient, but she was beyond commonsense.

Her attack was so unexpected he lost his balance and fell backwards, vanishing entirely into the hawthorn hedge. His language was so appalling her ears burned. She didn't wait for him to extricate himself, she turned and fled, towing her horse behind her. Fortunately she had only run a few yards when she spotted a tree stump ideal to use as a mounting block. She scrambled aboard, rammed her foot into the single iron, gathered up the reins and shouted at Firebrand to go. He went. He didn't like the crashing and shouting that was coming from the hedge any more than she did. Too late she remembered the ditch, but her horse was better prepared than she, and he gathered himself and sailed over. Emma remained perched precariously, but still in the saddle. Her gloves were slippery from the mud which meant she was having difficulty holding the reins and her bottom was sliding dangerously around on the saddle for the same reason. She had to rely on the horse's commonsense because she knew she was in no position to pull him up when they reached the yard.

The horse dropped to a trot and then a long easy walk before he emerged onto the gravel drive. He needed no urging to turn and head under the arch into the yard. Emma shouted to the grooms gawping in amazement at her sudden arrival.

'Quickly, he's coming, don't let him get me. He caused me to fall and now is blaming me for his predicament. Do something, Roberts, don't let him get in here.'

Roberts shouted and suddenly the yard was full of men. He ordered them to form a solid wall, their arms linked, across the entrance whilst he helped her from the saddle. 'You took no harm, Miss Meadows?'

'No, as you see, I'm no more than muddied. If Firebrand had not reacted so quickly I should have been killed as would the other rider and his horse. I know I shouldn't have gone out alone on him, but after my experience this morning I'm certain I can trust him with my life.'

She cowered in the loose box with her mount not wishing to be anywhere near Lord Denver when he arrived baying for her blood. She heard the sound of raised voices, then the clatter of hooves and the unexpected sound of laughter outside the box.

Roberts came in grinning. 'You're quite right, Miss Meadows, the man is deranged. He looked at us and laughed. Then he said something right peculiar. It was a message for you. 'Tell Miss Meadows to expect me this afternoon, we have unfinished business.' It's a puzzle to me how a complete stranger should know your name.'

Emma felt her breakfast threaten to return. She swallowed vigorously. 'I must go in and change. Thank you for your assistance, please see that Firebrand has extra feed.'

She decided to take the side door, she had no wish to be seen covered in mud and hear the exclamations of horror and concern from her grandmother. She crept in carefully, removing her boots, not wishing to cover the recently polished floor with her muddy footprints. She thought there was a back stairs for the servants' use somewhere along here.

A parlour maid came out of one of the closed doors and looked at her with horror. Emma quickly forestalled her queries. 'Yes, I took a tumble, but I'm fine as you can see. I wish you to take me to my apartment and then please order a bath to be sent up at once.'

It was going to take more than a hot soak to soothe her nerves; she fully understood the significance of Richard's message. He was coming later today when she would get her just desserts. She deserved to be chastised for having the temerity to strike him, but was worried that his message might contain some kind of veiled threat. She could think of only one thing he could do to her that would be unacceptable: insist that she gave up riding Firebrand, and she wasn't going to do that for anyone — even the man she loved.

11

Richard's fury had abated by the time he reached the stables into which his quarry had flown. He had to admit for a novice she had an excellent seat, and had taken the ditch like an expert horsewoman. He was almost prepared to admit that the massive chestnut gelding, although far too big and strong for her, suited her to perfection. His lips curved as he visualised her like an avenging Valkyrie, glorious red hair tumbling over her shoulders, her face streaked with mud, flinging abuse at him. His smile slipped a little and he raised a hand gingerly to touch his eye. He winced. His beloved certainly knew how to pack a punch, he would have to make sure he didn't infuriate her too often or he would be walking around with permanent black eyes. He laughed out loud at the thought and Black

Night, already overexcited by all the galloping and shouting experienced that morning shied violently and he almost took a nose dive into the hedge for a second time.

Mitchell was waiting for him at the Green Man and wisely refrained from commenting on his dishevelled appearance, scratched face and rapidly closing eye. 'What time would you be wanting the carriage, my lord?'

'I shall leave here at half past two exactly.'

'Yes, my lord, the carriage will be harnessed and waiting for you.'

His valet, Enderby, was not so reticent in his comments. 'Been in the wars, my lord? I hope the other fellow looks worse than you.'

'Enough. I shall not explain myself to you, just get me something to eat and make sure my bath is ready when I'm finished.' Richard could hear his servant sniggering as he left the room to bring up his mid-day meal. Normally he didn't eat at lunchtime but all the excitement had given him an appetite.

He spent longer on his appearance than he had done before. It was not just Emma he wished to impress but her wealthy grandparents. He had heard a lot about Sir James Masterson since he'd come into his title, all of it complimentary, about the man's first rate business brain and his probity. It wouldn't do to appear as anything other than his new persona. Richard Tennent, the rough soldier, must not be in evidence.

Satisfied at last his cravat was tied perfectly, his new jacket from Weston's fitted him as it should, his britches were smooth and his Hessians so shiny he could see his face in them, he headed down to the yard where his smart travelling carriage was waiting. He paused to admire the turnout. The four matching bays were obviously prime goers, and his coachman and outrider were immaculate in their bottle-green livery. But if everything was as it should be, why did he feel so nervous? Good grief — he'd faced Boney's troops with more equanimity. He jumped into the coach and settled back, patting his waistcoat pocket to check the ring box was still safely inside. He had been so sure that Emma returned his feelings he had purchased an emerald betrothal ring whilst seeing his brother on to the ship that was to take him to India.

★ ★ ★

'Do sit down, my dear girl, you are making my head spin with your marching round the room.' Sir James waved towards the chair next to his and reluctantly Emma came over and perched beside him.

'I do hope Lord Denver is not late; it has been hard enough trying to remain calm without having to wait after three o'clock for him to arrive.'

'It is five minutes to the hour, and if I'm not mistaken I have just seen a smart vehicle turn into the gates; my word, this young man of yours has a good eye for a horse and no mistake.'

Emma was back on her feet and across to the window before he could prevent her. She knew she would look ridiculous if he saw her peering round the edge of the window, but she wanted to be sure it was him. She recognized the bays and the coach as the ones that had transported her and her sister to the ill-fated party two weeks ago.

'Yes, Grandpapa, I recognize the horses as Denver's. Thank goodness the modiste and her assistant arrived this afternoon to take the measurements for Eugenie's new wardrobe, I couldn't bear to have Grand . . . ' As soon as the words were uttered she knew she had been disrespectful and blushed crimson. Her grandfather chuckled at her embarrassment.

'No, do not be discomposed, my love. I love my wife dearly, but I too am relieved she is not present for this delicate meeting.'

Eventually the front door knocker

sounded and Emma heard Foster bid Richard enter. She stood next to Sir James, one hand gripping tightly to a chair back in order to remain upright.

'Lord Denver to see you and Miss Meadows, Sir James.' The butler stood back and bowed him in.

Whatever she had been going to say was forgotten when she saw the discoloration of his eye and the dozens of deep lacerations to his cheeks.

'Richard, I cannot bear to see you so wounded, and all of it my fault.'

She didn't wait for him to answer. Forgetting that they were not alone in the drawing-room, she ran forward and threw herself into his arms. She reached up to stroke his cheeks, her eyes brimming with happiness that he was there and shame to have been the cause of his injuries.

'My darling, I have no one to blame but myself. I could have killed us both by my stupidity as you so rightly said. That horse of yours has my undying affection. Without his steadiness I might have lost the thing I prize above all others.'

Neither of them heard Sir James move past them and quietly close the door behind him as he left them alone. Richard dropped to one knee, taking her hands to his lips. The passion in his eyes, the love with which he kissed her knuckles was almost too much to bear.

'Emma, I love you to distraction. Will you do me the inestimable honour of becoming my wife?'

'Of course I will, my darling, but do get up and stop making a cake of yourself.'

At these bracing words he jumped to his feet and gathered her close. She could feel his heart pounding against hers and tilted her face to receive her first real kiss. A satisfying ten minutes later she stepped away, her eyes sparkling, her lips rosy. She led him to the love seat by the window.

'There's so much I wish to tell you, but I cannot find the words.'

'We don't need words, sweetheart, I

know how you are feeling for I am experiencing the same joy as you.' He reached in to his pocket and flipped open the ring box. 'This is for you, darling. It matches your eyes to perfection.'

Holding out her hand she watched him slide the ring over her knuckle and she knew that with that token their love and lives were irrevocably joined together.

THE END

We do hope that you have enjoyed reading this large print book.

Did you know that all of our titles are available for purchase?

We publish a wide range of high quality large print books including:
Romances, Mysteries, Classics General Fiction Non Fiction and Westerns

Special interest titles available in large print are:
The Little Oxford Dictionary Music Book, Song Book Hymn Book, Service Book

Also available from us courtesy of Oxford University Press:
Young Readers' Dictionary (large print edition) Young Readers' Thesaurus (large print edition)

For further information or a free brochure, please contact us at:
**Ulverscroft Large Print Books Ltd., The Green, Bradgate Road, Anstey, Leicester, LE7 7FU, England.
Tel:** (00 44) 0116 236 4325
Fax: (00 44) 0116 234 0205

FALLING LEAVES

Sheila Benton

When Richard employs Annie to update the computer system for his company, she finds herself, through circumstance, living in his house. Although they are attracted to each other, Richard's daughter, Katie, takes a dislike to her. Added to this, Annie suspects that Richard is in love with someone else, so she allows herself to be drawn to Steve, Richard's accountant. Annie feels she must choose between love and a career — how can the complications in her life be resolved . . . ?

ENCHANTED VOYAGE

Mavis Thomas

Lauren was a reluctant member of the family holiday group on a sea cruise, taking in Italy, Greece and Turkey. All her thoughts were of him: she agonised over Grant's accident, his operation, and his forthcoming marriage — to Elaine . . . However, whilst on the *Bella Italia*, Lauren became deeply involved with a charismatic member of the enter- tainment team . . . and a fellow passenger — a teacher and his two difficult children . . .

WHERE THE BLUEBELLS GROW WILD

Wendy Kremer

Stephen employs Sara, a landscape designer, to improve the appearance of the gardens of Knowles House, his Georgian mansion. He wants to use innovative ideas to generate additional sources of income and is hoping to hire it out for special events — an attractive garden would boost his chances. Lucy, Stephen's childhood friend, lives with her father on the adjoining country estate. Everyone thinks Lucy and Stephen are made for each other — but then along comes Sara . . .

THE BUTTERFLY DANCE

Rosemary A. Smith

It's 1902 and life, for Katherine Johnson, has been rather mundane, living with her Aunt Phoebe and Uncle Zachariah in their house on the coast. However, on her twentieth birthday, she meets Kane O'Brien on the beach and suddenly her thoughts are all of him. But will the circumstances of Kane's birth prevent her Aunt from accepting their love for one another? What is the mystery of the beautiful keepsake box? And where will the butterfly dance lead them?

LONG SHADOWS

Margaret Mounsdon

When Fiona Dalrymple's grand-mother dies, Fiona is shocked to learn that Doreen wasn't actually her grandmother at all . . . Her grandfather's first wife, Ellie Marsden, is still alive and when Fiona meets her, Ellie has a further shock for Fiona: she also has a brother. What's more, Tim has disappeared and Fiona is charged with the task of finding him . . . so why does Rory, Tim's handsome boss, seems intent on being more of a hindrance than a help?

LEAVING HOME

Cara Cooper

Flora Canning's bags are packed. She's ready to begin a fresh life in New York, leaving her handsome friend Richard Cross devastated at her departure. But plans don't always work out, and a family tragedy forces Flora to stay a while longer. Then fabulously wealthy Nate Campbell enters her life with an offer most women couldn't refuse, and Flora has to learn who to trust and whether it is better to rule with your head or with your heart.